Angel Food
for
Boys & Girls

Volume I

"Angel Food for Jack and Jill"
Little Talks to Young Folks

Father Gerald T. Brennan

Neumann Press
Charlotte, North Carolina

Nihil Obstat:
James C. McAniff
Censor Deputatus

Imprimatur:
✠ James E. Kearney
Bishop of Rochester

Rochester, New York, March 15, 1950

ISBN 978-0-911845-66-2

Printed and bound in the United States of America.

Neumann Press
Charlotte, North Carolina
www.NeumannPress.com
2013

Contents

Angel Food
for
Boys & Girls

Volume I

1. The Devil at the Door

LAST TUESDAY NIGHT the devil rang my doorbell. Yes, children, that's true! The devil rang my doorbell. I saw the devil and I even talked to him. Now I know you're surprised. Well, I was surprised, too. Let me tell you what happened!

I was reading the evening paper and, all of a sudden, the doorbell rang. Well, I hurried to the front door and opened it. And was I surprised? There on the front porch stood a little devil, a devil with horns on his head, a devil with evil eyes and grinding teeth. The devil wore a red coat and red pants, and he had a long, black tail. When the devil saw me, he growled. I waited for the devil to speak but he just growled and moaned.

Finally, I asked a question. "What do you want, Mr. Devil?" and I wondered what he was going to say.

"This is Little Devils' Night," he said in a low voice. "This is Halloween. Tricks or treat?"

Well, I didn't want the devil to play any tricks on me, so I told him that I'd treat him. I invited the devil into my office and he sat on a chair. Can you imagine the devil sitting in my office? What else could I do? I had to be nice to him.

I treated the devil to a bottle of Coca-Cola and a couple of sandwiches. I guess the devil didn't have any supper, because he was certainly hungry and he finished the sandwiches and drink in no time. But do you know, children, the devil never took off his false face. He raised it a little and I tried to find out just who he was, but the devil was foxy. He didn't want me to know, and he was very careful to keep his face covered.

The devil was pleased with his treat but I wanted to make sure. So, I filled a bag with apples, oranges, walnuts, bananas, and a few candy bars. He was certainly a polite devil, because he thanked me and started for the door.

"Who are you, anyway?" I asked the devil before he left. "What's your name?"

"Guess!" he answered very quickly.

Well, I guessed and guessed while the devil shook his head. I mentioned the names of several boys in our school but every time I was wrong. Maybe the devil was a girl. How could I tell? No, sir! I couldn't guess the devil's name and he wouldn't tell me.

"Thanks, Father, for a swell treat!" said the devil as he walked down the steps. "I must ring more doorbells before it gets too late."

And the devil disappeared in the darkness.

When I went back to my room last Tuesday night, I thought about the devil for a long time. Who was that devil? What was his name? What boy or girl pretended that he or she was the devil? I wondered and wondered. And I wondered, too, about all the other boys and girls who were pretending that night, boys and girls who were wearing false faces. Some were pretending that they were cowboys, robbers, witches, and ghosts. Others were pretending that they were nurses and old ladies. Halloween is a great night, you know, for pretenders, a night when boys and girls pretend to be what they are not, a night when boys and girls wear false faces. When Halloween is over, off come the false faces.

That little devil, whoever he was, certainly kept his secret. He didn't want me to know and I didn't find out who he was. I don't know yet who rang my doorbell, and I don't suppose that I will ever know the name of that devil. But there is one Person from whom that devil didn't keep his secret, and that Person is God. That devil fooled me, but he didn't fool God, because God sees everything and He knows everything. Why, God looked right under the devil's false face and He knew the child's name. That devil pretended and fooled a good many people last Tuesday night, but he didn't fool God. And God knew the names of all the other boys and girls who pretended on Halloween, because God knows everything. God sees everything.

Children, there are many boys and girls who don't wait until Halloween to pretend. They wear false faces every day. When these children are in school, they pretend to be very good, but when they are home or with other children, they are sometimes bad. They disobey at home and talk back to their parents. Sometimes they even lie to their fathers and mothers. When they are with other children, they steal, cheat, and say bad words. These children are pretenders. They wear false faces. These children fool the priests and Sisters and even their parents, but they don't fool God. No, sir! God is watching them every minute. God sees everything they do.

It's a good thing to remember that God is always on the job and that He never misses anything. When you do something good, you know that God sees it and that He will reward you. When you're tempted to do wrong, just remember that God has His eye on you, and that thought will help you to keep away from sin.

Boys and girls, you know what is right and what is wrong. Do the right thing every time because God sees you! Don't be a pretender! Don't wear a false face!

2. Three Farms

THERE WAS ONCE a great King who was very kind. This King loved his people and he was very good to them. He loved, especially, the poor. The King built hospitals, schools, and playgrounds for the poor. He even visited their homes and tried to make them happy.

Now, one day the King had an unusual idea. He ordered twenty of his soldiers to search the kingdom. He wanted the soldiers to find three men, three men who were very poor, three men whose families were suffering. When the soldiers found the three men, they were to bring them to the King.

The soldiers obeyed orders and began their search. For months they visited every city and town. They visited the homes of the poor and talked with men, women, and children. They wrote in their books what they saw and heard, and, finally, the soldiers finished their work. Yes, after months of searching, the soldiers found three men who were very poor, three men whose families were suffering. So, the soldiers brought the three men to the King.

"My friends," said the kind King, "I have brought

you here today because I want to help you. I'm going to give each of you a new start in life. I'm going to give each of you a house and a farm. If you work hard on your farm, someday, you'll be rich and happy."

Of course, the three men were surprised and delighted. They thanked the King for his great kindness and each man promised that he would work hard. Each man wanted to show the King that he was grateful.

Many people, you know, make promises and some people keep their promises. Did the three men work hard and keep the promises they made to the King? Well, the King often wondered about the three men and their farms, but he never asked any questions. Finally, after six years the King decided that he would find out whether the men kept their promises. The King decided to visit the three farms.

The King went to the first farm and what do you think he found? He found that the man on the first farm had done no work at all. The man hadn't plowed or planted, and the grass and weeds were growing high. The man hadn't taken care of the trees, so there was no fruit. The barn was not painted and the fences were broken. Even the house had been neglected. The house needed paint, the roof leaked, and some of the windows were broken. When the King saw the first farm, he was sad and disappointed.

When the King visited the second farm, he was

disappointed again. The second farm was almost as bad as the first one. The man on the second farm had worked the first year. Then he tired, and he didn't work any more. The man forgot about his promise to the King, and when the man didn't work, his farm suffered.

I suppose you are wondering what the King found on the third farm. Well, on the third farm the King had a pleasant surprise. He found vegetables growing in the garden, and he saw fields of oats, wheat, and hay. The King found trees loaded with apples, pears, peaches, and plums. He saw horses, cows, pigs, and chickens. And the King smiled when he saw the beautiful home and the well-kept barn. You can be sure that the King didn't have to ask any questions. The King knew that the man on the third farm had worked hard. He knew that the man was making money and that he was happy. The man on the third farm had kept his promise.

Now, that isn't the end of the story. Each year on the first day of March, the man on the third farm received a mysterious box. Sometimes, there was gold in the box. Other times there was silver. Once there was a diamond. And the man on the third farm never knew who sent the mysterious box. But I know that the mysterious box came from the King as a reward to a man who had done his job well.

Children, God is our King and a very kind King, too. He loves every one of us and He wants us to be happy forever. Like the King in the story, God has given each one of us a gift — He has given us a soul. God wants us to take good care of that soul. He wants us to work for that soul every day. God wants us to pray and to receive the Sacraments. He wants us to keep His laws. If we neglect our soul, we will never be happy. If we take care of our soul, God will reward us.

There are many people in this world today who act like the man on the first farm. They do nothing for their souls. They never pray: they never go to confession or receive Holy Communion: they never go to Mass. Yes, they even break God's laws. Surely, these people can't expect God to reward them.

Other people act like the man on the second farm. They work for their souls for a while. Then they get tired and quit. They forget all about God and their souls. Do you think that God will reward them? I don't think so!

Boys and girls, I hope you are like the man on the third farm. I hope you work for your soul every day by saying your prayers, keeping God's laws, and receiving the Sacraments. As long as you live, you must never stop doing these things. If you take good care of your soul, God will keep His eye on you. He will bless you with happiness and success. God will reward you, not once a year, but forever. Your reward will not be diamonds, or silver, or gold. Your reward will be better than all these things — God will give you heaven.

3. Football Johnny

IF I WERE TO ASK you what you are going to be when you grow up, you would all give me a different answer. You would tell me that you want to be a priest or a doctor or a lawyer. Perhaps you want to be a plumber or a policeman. Maybe a girl wants to be a nurse or a teacher. Oh, you would all have different answers. Every child feels that he knows right now just what he is going to be when he grows up. Well, that's the way it was with Johnny Clark. When Johnny was a boy, he wanted to be a football player, not an ordinary football player, but a great football player. Johnny wanted to be a star.

Johnny liked all kinds of sports, but his favorite game was football. Why, Johnny even had a football of his own. During the summer when other boys played baseball, Johnny played football. That's why his friends called him, "Football Johnny."

When Johnny went to high school, he didn't have much time for football because he had to study hard. Of course, he played some football, but not as much as he wished. He tried out for the team, but he didn't make it. So, Johnny had to watch the football games from the grandstand.

Then Johnny went to college. He worked hard at his studies, and he worked hard at his football, too. Every afternoon Johnny was out on the football field. He practiced and practiced and practiced. And what do you think? Johnny made the team. Every day he worked hard at practice and followed the coach's orders. Johnny wanted to be a good player; in fact, he wanted to be the best player on the team.

Johnny, however, was not the best player on the football team. There were too many boys who could play better than Johnny, and every Saturday afternoon it was the same story. The coach wouldn't let Johnny play, and every Saturday Johnny sat on the bench. Johnny just wasn't good enough to play against a strong team. That's what the coach thought, and I don't have to tell you that Johnny felt pretty bad about it.

Johnny tried not to show his feelings. He was heartbroken, and all that he wanted was a chance to play, a chance to prove that he could play well. The coach, however, never gave Johnny that chance.

It was the last game of the season and an important game, too. Before the game, Johnny went to the coach. "Please, coach," he begged, "let me play in this game!"

The coach shook his head. "No, Johnny," he answered, "I can't take any chances. I want to win this game."

"Please, please," begged Johnny again. "I've got to play in this game. Give me a chance!"

10

The coach thought for a moment. "All right," he said, "I'll let you play for the first three minutes, but no longer. I must win this game."

Johnny was delighted and his heart pounded within him. At last, at last, he was going to play. He was going to play in a big game even though it would only be for three minutes.

Now, this will surprise you. Do you know that Johnny played so well during those three minutes that the coach left him in the game? Why, Johnny played so well that the coach couldn't believe his eyes. Johnny was all over that field. He blocked and he tackled. He threw the ball and caught forward passes. And what do you think? Johnny even made a field goal.

Johnny Clark certainly surprised everybody. He played better than any man on his team. And after Johnny's team won the game, the other players carried Johnny on their shoulders. Johnny was a hero, the hero of the day, the star of the game.

When the coach met Johnny in the clubhouse, he shook the boy's hand. "Johnny," said the coach, "you were wonderful. You played a great game. How did you do it?"

"Coach," answered the young hero, "my father was in the grandstand today, and it was the first time he ever saw me play. I knew my father was watching me. So, I just had to be good."

Children, do you know that you are very much like Johnny Clark? You, too, are in a contest, a contest that takes place every single day. You are trying to get your soul into heaven, and the devil is playing against you. Every day you must try to do something good even though the devil tries to knock you down. If you want to win heaven, you must fight hard and you must fight the devil. No one ever wins a game by taking it easy, and you won't win heaven unless you work.

Why did Johnny Clark play so well? Because his father was watching him! God, your Father, is watching you, too. He sees everything you do. He hears every word you speak. Wherever you go, God is with you. That's why you should make good use of every minute. God is watching you and He is keeping score. Every good play you make, every temptation you fight, God sees, and God gives you credit for everything. That's a good thing to know and a good thing to remember. You are never alone, because God is always with you. Shouldn't that thought make you work harder and harder for heaven? Well, it certainly should. When boys and girls forget that God is watching, then, they do wrong.

Children, God wants you to play a good game in life. He wants you to come out on top and save your soul. Remember, God is on your side. He is watching every play. God wants you to be a winner.

4. The Dog That Didn't Want a Vacation

EDDIE CRAMER had a dog whose name was Shag. Like all boys who own a dog, Eddie was very fond of Shag. The boy taught the little collie many tricks, and the dog liked to perform for Eddie and his friends. Naturally, Eddie was very proud of his little friend.

Every day Shag followed Eddie to school. Of course, the dog couldn't go into the school with his master, but Shag waited outside on the school steps. When school was over, Shag was always on the steps, waiting for his friend, Eddie. The dog even followed the boy to church on Sundays. He would wait outside the church, and after Mass, the two friends would walk home together. So you can see that Eddie and Shag were pretty good friends.

Last summer, when Eddie's father announced that he was going to drive the family to California for a vacation, there was plenty of excitement. Eddie liked the idea of riding from Albany to California, but his first thoughts were about the dog. What about

Shag? Would he have to stay home? Who would feed him? Who would give him a drink? The dog certainly couldn't stay home alone.

Eddie begged his father to let Shag make the trip, but his father wouldn't listen. The father felt that the trip would be too much for the dog. He felt the dog would need too much care. But that wasn't the way Eddie felt about Shag. Eddie begged and teased his father to let the dog go and, finally, the father gave in. Eddie was happy because Shag was going to California with him.

At first Shag seemed to enjoy the trip. He was full of life and very playful, but after a few days, the dog seemed to lose his pep. He was tired of traveling and wanted to go home. Most of the time Shag slept on the floor of the car and refused to eat. There was something wrong with Shag and Eddie began to worry.

The Cramers were traveling through Colorado and they decided to spend the night in a house by the side of the road. Again Shag refused to eat any supper. So, Eddie fixed a blanket for a bed, and the dog went to sleep on the side porch of the house.

When Eddie awoke in the morning, his first thought was about Shag. He dressed and ran down to the porch. And what do you think? Shag wasn't there. The dog was gone. Well, Eddie called the dog and searched everywhere, but there was no Shag. The dog had disappeared.

Eddie Cramer's heart was broken and he didn't

enjoy the rest of the trip. Eddie had lost his best friend and he found it hard to be happy. Even though the Cramers did have an exciting time in California, Eddie's good time was spoiled. Eddie had lost his dog. Shag was gone. It was a hard blow to little Eddie.

After spending six weeks in California, the Cramers started for home. It was a long trip across the country, a lonesome trip for Eddie. Time and time again the boy thought about his dog and wondered what had happened to him. Eddie knew that he would never see Shag again.

The Cramers were home about two months and Eddie was back at school. One afternoon Eddie marched out of school with the other children. And what do you think? There on the school steps sat a dog. Eddie could hardly believe his eyes. Yes, the dog was Shag. Eddie's dog was alive and safe. Shag had walked all the way home from Colorado.

Eddie lifted the dog from the steps, held him in his arms, and hurried home. Even though Shag had run away, Eddie forgave him. Of course, Shag was very tired, very thin, and very hungry. Eddie, however, took care of everything, and that night, Shag had the best meal that he had had in weeks. And that isn't all! The dog went to bed on a soft, clean blanket and slept soundly.

Now I don't have to tell you that Eddie Cramer was happy. I'm pretty sure that Shag was happy, too. Shag got into lots of trouble and suffered a great deal during all those weeks, but he learned a lesson. Never again would Shag run away from his master.

Sometimes, boys and girls run away from their Master. They run away from God, and they stay away from God for a long, long time. They don't say their prayers. They don't go to confession or receive Holy Communion. They even miss Mass and fall into mortal sin. Like Shag, these boys and girls get into trouble and are not happy. Boys and girls can't be happy when they are away from God.

If you should ever run away from God, don't stay away too long! If you should ever fall into mortal sin, go back to God as soon as you can. No matter how many times you run away from God, He is always ready to take you back. God is always ready to forgive you. He is always patient and very kind.

God never shuts the door on anybody. He hates sin, but He loves sinners, especially, when they come back to Him. God knows that little children need Him. That's why He is always so kind to them.

Children, if you ever make the mistake of running away from God, go back to Him quickly! How can you go back to God? Go to confession!

5. 123,456 Mosquitoes

MANY CHILDREN have a hobby — something they do during their spare time — and some of these hobbies are very interesting. Some children save stamps, buttons, coins, old bottles, toy elephants, and toy dogs. Others make things during their spare time. They build dollhouses, boats, and bridges, and of course, some girls sew, knit, and bake cakes.

The other day, children, I heard about a man who had a very strange hobby. Now you'll laugh when you hear about this man's hobby because this man collected mosquitoes. Yes, the man was a famous doctor, and during his spare time, the doctor collected mosquitoes.

Now, I can't tell you just how the doctor caught the mosquitoes, but he caught them just the same, and he caught them alive. What did the doctor do with the mosquitoes? Well, he put them in a box. It was a very large box and the box was lined with cotton. The doctor, you know, wanted his mosquitoes to be comfortable, and he wanted them to have a soft bed at night. He felt that, if he was kind to the mosquitoes, the mosquitoes would be kind, too, and they wouldn't sting people any more. Every day the doctor fed the mosquitoes plenty of syrup and rich milk. He kept the mosquitoes cool in the summer with an electric fan, and on cold winter nights he kept them warm by covering the box with a blanket. Of course, the mosquitoes liked their home. They liked the syrup, the rich milk, the electric fan, the warm blanket, and the grand cotton bed where they slept at night.

The doctor collected mosquitoes for seven long years and during that time he collected 123,456 mosquitoes. Yes, there were 123,456 mosquitoes in the big box and they were all alive. Every day 123,456 mosquitoes feasted on syrup and rich milk, and every night 123,456 mosquitoes went to sleep on a soft cotton bed.

One day the doctor invited some famous people to come to his home. He invited kings, presidents, soldiers, doctors, lawyers, and bankers, and these famous men came from all parts of the world. Of course, no one knew why the doctor had invited them.

"Gentlemen," said the doctor as he stood before his famous guests, "I have in this box 123,456 mosquitoes. I have been kind to these mosquitoes for seven long years. I have fed them syrup and rich milk every day, and I have put them to sleep at night on a grand bed of soft cotton. These mosquitoes are friendly mosquitoes, and they won't sting."

When the doctor finished, he opened the large box and out came 123,456 mosquitoes.

"Don't be afraid!" smiled the doctor. "The mosquitoes are friendly and they won't harm you."

But those 123,456 mosquitoes didn't spend much time flying around that room. Those mosquitoes didn't want to fly. They wanted to sit. And where do you think the mosquitoes sat? Right on the heads, necks, and hands of the famous men. Of course, the men were nervous but they tried to sit still. But they only sat still for a few moments. Suddenly, there was a terrible commotion.

"Ouch!" cried the famous men at the top of their voices as 123,456 mosquitoes began to bite and sting.

The men slapped their heads. They slapped their necks. They waved their hands, and they ran from the room.

I suppose you are wondering about the doctor who had been so kind to the mosquitoes. Did the mosquitoes bother the doctor? Well, the mosquitoes certainly did bother the doctor. The mosquitoes stung the doctor just as they stung the famous men. And that day the doctor and his famous guests learned a very important lesson: *Never trust a mosquito!*

Mosquitoes are very small insects. Why, they're so small that sometimes you can't even see them. You don't even know that the mosquitoes are around until they bite or sting you. Then it's too late to do anything. After a mosquito bites, you just have to suffer. Don't ever get the idea that mosquitoes are friendly! Even though they have been brought up on syrup and rich milk, they'll sting you every time. So never trust a mosquito!

Boys and girls, there is someone else whom you should never trust and that's the devil. Like the mosquito, you'll never see the devil and you'll never know that he is around, but he is around you just the same. The devil follows you wherever you go and he is always waiting for a chance to sting you, to lead you into sin, to make you suffer. And don't think that you can be friendly with the devil, because he will harm you every time he gets a chance. That's the way the devil works. He doesn't like you, and you shouldn't like him. When the devil tempts you, run away from him just as you run away from a tiny mosquito! If you don't run from the devil, you'll fall into sin.

The devil is a foxy fellow, a bad fellow, and he has lots of tricks. He wants you to lose your soul. He wants your soul for himself. He wants your soul to go to hell. That's why he tempts you. That's why he tries to lead you into sin. Remember, he is fighting for your soul every minute. When the devil bothers you, chase him away by saying a prayer! A prayer will chase the devil every time.

Children, be on your guard! *Never trust the devil, and never trust a mosquito!*

6. Peanuts and Watermelon

CHICHI WAS A MONKEY, a little brown monkey that lived in a cage. Of course, Chichi had a very good home with plenty to eat, but just the same the little monkey was not happy. Chichi didn't like to live in a cage. Like all monkeys, he wanted to be free. But there was nothing that Chichi could do about it. Chichi was a prisoner, a prisoner in a cage with a big lock on the door.

One day, however, Chichi's master forgot to lock the door of the cage. That was just what the little monkey wanted. When no one was looking, Chichi opened the door of the cage and ran down the street as fast as he could. Boy, was that monkey happy? Chichi was free. He was a prisoner no longer. At last, the monkey could do just as he pleased.

Chichi ran only a short distance when he saw an open window. He jumped through the window and climbed into bed with twelve-year-old Dickie Cowan. Dickie screamed, and Chichi dashed through the house, knocked over a lamp, and ran to the garage. There he turned on the water faucet, spilled a bucket of paint, and ate a bunch of grapes that he found in a basket. After eating the grapes, Chichi once again ran down the street and he certainly caused plenty of excitement. Children laughed and clapped when they saw the monkey, but women screamed and called for help. Several boys tried to catch the little fellow, but Chichi was too smart for them. A policeman tried to coax him, but Chichi climbed up a pole and refused to come down. Oh, how the monkey laughed and chattered to himself! No policeman was going to catch Chichi. No, sir, not if he could help it.

When the policeman went away, Chichi came down the pole. "I think I'll find a good hiding place," he said to himself as he hurried down the street.

Chichi was very careful because he didn't want to get caught. When he saw anyone coming toward him, he ran into a yard and hid. Then, when the stranger passed, the monkey left his hiding place and moved along. Finally, Chichi came to the end of the street, and there he found just what he wanted — a great, big yard with a large tree at the end of the yard. Then and there, Chichi decided to spend the night in the tree. He was sure that no one would see him there.

Chichi was wrong. Someone did see the little monkey. The next morning, when Mr. Corcoran went to his tool shed, he saw the monkey up in the tree.

"That monkey would make a fine pet for my little boy," said the man to himself and he began to think.

Now Mr. Corcoran didn't know very much about catching monkeys, and he wondered just how he would go about it. He thought and thought for a long time. Then he had an idea. You'll never guess what Mr. Corcoran decided to do. He put a plate of peanuts and watermelon right under the tree and then went into the house.

Well, when Chichi saw the peanuts and watermelon, his eyes almost popped out of his head. He hurried down from his hiding place and did he have a feast! Why, that monkey was a champion eater of peanuts and watermelon and in no time the peanuts and watermelon were gone. When the party was over, Chichi went back to his place in the tree and soon he was fast asleep.

The next day Chichi found more peanuts and more watermelon, and, of course, he had another feast. This went on for several days. Each morning the monkey found more peanuts and watermelon waiting for him, and each morning the monkey had a feast.

Now there was one thing that Chichi didn't know. He didn't notice that, each day, the peanuts and watermelon were placed just a little closer to the door of the tool shed. Finally, one day Mr. Corcoran put the peanuts and watermelon just inside the door of the shed. Then he tied a long string to the screen door and, hiding behind a tree, he held the end of the string tightly. As long as Mr. Corcoran held the string tightly, the door remained open.

When Chichi hurried through the door for his morning meal, Mr. Corcoran loosened the string.

The door slammed and once again, Chichi was a prisoner, a prisoner in the tool shed. The monkey was caught. Chichi had walked right into the trap, and he found out too late that the peanuts and watermelon were only bait.

That's just the way the devil works. He sets traps for little boys and girls. The devil pretends that he is your friend, and sometimes he pretends for a long, long time. He tempts you and makes you think that sin is something nice. Then, all of a sudden, the devil catches you in his trap and you fall into sin.

The devil wants you. He wants every one of you and he wants to steal you away from God. The devil knows that sin is the only thing that will take you away from God. That's why he tries so hard to get you to fall into sin. The devil is a sly fellow and he uses some very clever tricks. So, you have to be on guard at all times.

When temptations come, fight hard against them! If you pray, you won't fall into sin. Remember, temptations are traps. If you pray when you are tempted, you won't get caught. Remember, too, that the devil never gets tired and he never gives up. He keeps right after you because he wants your soul. Don't be fooled by the devil! Don't get caught in his trap!

7. The Brightest Star

DO YOU KNOW that there are millions of stars in the sky? Yes, there are! Some stars are very large and shine brightly. Other stars are very small and can't be seen at all. Now, this morning I want to tell you a story about a star, a star that was once the brightest star in the sky.

It seems that, when God made the stars, He made one star larger and brighter than all the rest, and He gave that star the first place in the sky. God put that brightest star right in the center of the sky. Of course, the Brightest Star knew that it was very important. In fact, the Star used to smile when other stars tried to outshine it. The Brightest Star knew that it was God's favorite, and no other star could take that honor from it.

Night after night the Brightest Star could be seen by people on this earth. Farmers, doctors, lawyers, sailors at sea, and little children looked up at the sky and admired the Star. It was always there. The Star was always shining brightly.

I suppose you know that on the night Jesus was born, all the stars tried to shine brighter than usual.

But none of the stars beat the Brightest Star. Why, on that first Christmas night the Brightest Star shone like a searchlight in the sky. It even lighted up the cave of Bethlehem for Jesus, Mary, and Joseph. Of course, God was pleased with the Brightest Star that night, and the Star was happy because it pleased God.

After that first Christmas night, however, the Brightest Star did something that did not please God. The Star became very proud. The Star knew that it was the best star in the sky, and it looked down on all the other stars. The Brightest Star wouldn't play with the other stars or even notice them. The smaller stars tried to be friendly, but the Brightest Star paid no attention to them.

Now God knows everything and He knew what His favorite star was doing. God wanted all of His stars to be friendly, but the Brightest Star spoiled everything. Well, God thought about the Brightest Star for a long, long time and then He decided to act. Do you know what God did to the Brightest Star? He punished it. First of all, God changed the Brightest Star into a very small star. Then He moved the star from the center and placed it away over in the corner of the sky. For hundreds of years that tiny star has remained in the corner of the sky. Night after night it has tried to shine brightly, but it is only a tiny speck in the sky, and most of the time it cannot be seen. The Star knows now that it made a terrible mistake. It would still be the Brightest

Star in the sky, but pride spoiled everything. That Star must remain as it is. Why? Because the Star was too proud.

Almighty God has a place in this world for each one of you children. He has given each one of you certain gifts, and to some He has given more gifts than to others. Everything you have has come from God. Never forget that! Now God wants you to use your gifts for His honor and glory. He doesn't want you to be proud. If you have more gifts and talents than other boys and girls, God wants you to be humble and He wants you to use your gifts in the right way. God doesn't want you to be a show-off.

Very often you will meet some boys and girls who act just like the Brightest Star. God has given them extra gifts and they feel that they are better than other boys and girls. If some boys or girls learn easily or get high marks in school or become the star of the class, what happens to them? They become proud and hold their heads up high. Now that's a sin! It's a sin of pride. Don't forget that God doesn't like proud people! God punished Satan because he was proud. God punished the Brightest Star because it was proud. If you are proud, God may punish you, too.

Don't ever get the idea that you are better than any of your companions! If you have a better home or wear finer clothes than your friends, you should thank God for being so good to you. If you can do things better or quicker than other children, it's because God has blessed you. Don't ever look down on your companions! Don't be proud! A proud child never has many friends. Remember, God likes each star just as He made it, and God likes you just as He made you.

The next time you are out at night, look up at the sky and see the beautiful stars! But don't try to look for that tiny Star in the corner of the sky, because you won't be able to find it. Let that tiny Star teach you a lesson — don't be proud!

8. The Angel With Silver Wings

IT WAS CHRISTMAS EVE in heaven. The angels had just finished preparing for the King's birthday and they were waiting for the great feast, waiting for the time when they would play their music and sing their songs.

Now, an angel with silver wings stood close to the throne of God. "I wonder what Christmas means to the people on earth," said the angel to some of his friends.

Almighty God heard the angel and called the angel aside. "You were wondering what Christmas means to the people on earth," said God to the angel with silver wings. "Christmas means many things to the people on earth. Many people have forgotten the real meaning of Christmas."

The angel was surprised, and God knew that the angel was disturbed. "I want you to go down to earth," said God to the angel. "I want you to find something for Me."

Of course, the angel didn't like the idea of leaving heaven on Christmas eve, but he agreed to go. And what do you think God wanted the angel to do? God wanted the angel to find one person on earth who knew the real meaning of Christmas.

It was a cold night to leave heaven, but the angel with silver wings flew quickly, and, in a short time, he was down on earth. He went directly to the city of Chicago because the angel felt that there he would find someone who knew the meaning of Christmas. Of course, no one saw the angel, but, as he hurried along, the angel saw many people. Some looked tired and others looked very happy. "Merry Christmas!" they called to one another, and the angel smiled.

The angel stopped to listen to children playing in the streets. He went to their homes. He felt that some child might know the meaning of Christmas. Finally, the angel found a boy, a boy by the name of Frank Murphy. Frank was happy because he had received so many fine presents, a bicycle, an electric train, a football, money, and some books. No wonder Frank was happy and excited. In the midst of his excitement, the angel heard Frank say: "I like Christmas because Christmas means lots of presents."

The angel was disappointed. He wrote in his little book the name of Frank Murphy and what Christmas meant to the little boy. To Frank Murphy Christmas meant lots of presents.

Then the angel went to a large store. The store was closed and the clerks had gone home. But the angel found the owner of the store sitting in his office. And what do you suppose the owner of the store was doing? He was counting his money. The owner smiled as he counted thousands of dollars, and when he finished, the owner spoke aloud. "Business was good this year. I made more money this Christmas than I did last year."

The angel heard the man and he wrote the man's name in his little book. To the owner of the store Christmas meant money, lots of money. Once again the angel was disappointed.

But the angel didn't give up his search. Oh, no! He was determined to find someone who knew the real meaning of Christmas. And what do you think? The angel met a little girl carrying a basket. So, the angel followed the child up a narrow stairs, down a long hall, and into a room. A blind lady sat in the corner.

"Here are some cookies!" said the girl to the blind lady. "Mother said that I must be kind at Christmas."

The angel didn't wait to hear any more. To the girl with the basket Christmas meant being kind to others.

It was almost midnight and the angel with silver wings hadn't yet found anyone who knew the real meaning of Christmas. The angel was tired and sad. Should he give up his search and go back to heaven? No, the angel decided to remain on earth. He felt sure that he would meet someone who knew the real meaning of Christmas.

The angel hurried along, and finally, he came to

a church. He entered the church and found a seat near the door. Oh, the church was beautiful with its flowers and lights. It was almost like heaven. Now the angel was happy. He was happy because he was in God's house. Once again the angel was close to God.

The Mass began and the choir sang. Then the priest turned to speak to the people. And what did the priest say? In simple words the priest told the world's greatest love story, the story of how Christ was born, the story of Bethlehem. The priest told how Jesus left His home in heaven and was born in a stable. He told about the shepherds who visited Jesus, and he told about the Three Kings. "God became Man on that first Christmas night," said the priest, "because He loves us. God came on earth to be near us, to show us the way to heaven. God came to teach us how to suffer. God came to die for us."

When the angel heard the priest's words, he smiled. At last the angel had found someone who knew the real meaning of Christmas. And when Mass was over, the angel hurried from the church and flew back to heaven.

The angel with silver wings told God everything that happened. He told God about Frank Murphy. He told about the man in the store. He told about the girl with the basket. When the angel told God about the priest, do you know what God did? God wrote the name of that priest with letters of gold in His great, big book. That priest knew the real meaning of Christmas.

Children, I think that by now you, too, know the real meaning of Christmas. God left heaven and became Man on Christmas day. He was born in a stable. His foster father was Joseph and His mother was Mary. God came on earth to suffer, to die on a cross, to open for us the gates of heaven. That, children, is the real meaning of Christmas.

9. A Mother for Easter

CARL THOMPSON was a little sad-eyed boy. Carl not only had sad eyes but he was sad inside. The boy was sad because he wanted something, and he wanted that something more than anything else in the world. Most of you boys and girls have what Carl wanted, and I can understand why the ten-year-old boy was always sad. Listen to his story!

Carl lived in a neat five-room house with his grandfather and grandmother. Both grandparents were very old, and, besides, his grandmother was very sick. The old people were good to the boy but they were poor, and they couldn't give him very much. But that really didn't bother Carl. What the boy wanted most of all was something that money cannot buy. Carl wanted his mother.

All the other children had mothers, mothers who lived with them, played with them, went to church with them, mothers who loved them, mothers whom they loved very much. Carl wished that he were like other children. He knew that life would be different if he only had his mother.

Many times the little boy thought about his

mother. He had never seen his mother and he wondered about her. Was his mother tall or short? Was she kind and pleasant? Could she sing? Could his mother tell stories? Could she make apple pie and chocolate cake? Why did his mother stay away? Why didn't she ever come to visit him? These and many more questions bothered the little boy and made him very unhappy. Oh, how he wished that things would change! Carl Thompson wanted his mother.

Well, one day Carl had an idea. It was the week before Easter and Carl decided to do something. Now you'll never guess what the little boy did, so I'll tell you. Carl wrote a letter. Yes, he wrote a letter to the newspaper and here's what the little boy said:

Dear Mister:

I am a little boy ten years old and my name is Carl Thompson. I am sending you my picture and I want you to put it in the paper. Everyone who has a mother has good luck, and I want my mother because my grandma is old and sick. Maybe my mother will see my picture in the paper and will come home for Easter. Please help me, Mister!

Your little friend,
Carl Thompson

Yes, the newspaperman put Carl's picture in the paper and thousands of people saw the picture and read about Carl. I suppose you are wondering whether Carl's mother saw the picture. Well, here's what happened!

While Carl was eating his breakfast on Easter

Sunday, the door opened and a very beautiful woman entered the room. Now I don't think that I have to tell you the rest of the story. Yes, the beautiful woman was the boy's mother, and Carl Thompson had his mother for Easter. And that isn't all! Carl still has his mother, and today that little boy is the happiest boy in this world. Carl Thompson is happy because he has his mother.

Boys and girls, we all have a mother, a very beautiful mother, the best mother in the world, the Blessed Virgin Mary. The Blessed Virgin belongs to each of us because Jesus gave her to us to be our mother. Mary loves us. She wants to be near us. She wants to help us save our souls.

Mary is always around to help us. Mary, you know, never leaves us, but once in a while, some boys and girls leave Mary. They run away from their mother because they think they can get along without her. Yes, boys and girls run away from Mary when they don't pray to her. Of course, when boys and girls act that way, Mary worries because she knows that children need her. Every mother worries about her children, and Mary doesn't want any of her children to get into trouble. So, don't you ever make the mistake of running away from Mary!

Children are always happy when they are with their mother. If you love Mary and keep close to her, you'll learn to hate sin, and you'll be the happiest boys and girls in this world. You can't love Mary and like sin, too. That's why Jesus wants you to keep close to Mary. He knows, that if you hate sin, you will save your soul.

Boys and girls, pray to Mary every day! Ask Mary to be a real mother to you! Ask her to watch over you and protect you and keep you from sin! Remember, Mary is your best friend and she will take you to Jesus, and that's what you want. It's a terrible thing to be without a mother, and it will be terrible for you if you don't keep Mary for your mother. Mary, the best mother in the world, wants you to keep close to her. Keep close to Mary by praying to her often!

10. A Box of Hail Marys

A LITTLE OLD LADY climbed up the steps of heaven. She was a tired old lady, because she had spent seventy-eight years on earth and had worked hard. She had raised a family and had suffered much. Yes, she was a tired old lady because she had just finished a long journey.

The old lady rang the bell and slowly the gates of heaven opened. An angel came to meet her.

"We have been looking for you," smiled the angel. "Come in and be happy forever!"

The woman passed through the gates of heaven and stopped to look. And was she surprised? She had never seen anything like heaven. Everything was so beautiful and everyone was so happy. Many times the old lady had thought about heaven and wondered what it is like. Now she knew. Now she was in heaven. She could hardly believe it.

The old lady walked a short distance and then she stopped to ask the angel some questions. "Why are all the other angels carrying packages? Where are they going?"

The angel smiled. "You have come to heaven on our Lady's birthday," he answered, "and the angels are bringing gifts to Mary."

"Oh, I can't stay," said the woman as she turned to leave. "My clothes are not very good and I have no present for Mary."

The angel begged her to say, but the woman shook her head. But just then a very beautiful woman came toward them. Yes, the beautiful woman was Mary, and the Blessed Virgin was very kind to the old lady.

Of course, the little old lady wished Mary a happy birthday. She told Mary that she was sorry that she didn't have better clothes. If she had known that it was Mary's birthday, she would certainly have brought a gift.

"Oh, but you did bring a gift," said the Blessed Virgin Mary. "Your gift came to heaven before you arrived."

The woman was puzzled. She didn't understand Mary's words. The woman didn't know anything about a gift, but she was sure that she had heard Mary say that a gift had arrived.

After some time, the angel gave the woman a beautiful robe. She put on the robe and I don't have to tell you that the little old lady was happy. Yes, she was very happy. But what do you think happened then? The angel led the little old lady to Mary's throne, and Mary placed a crown of gold on the lady's head, a crown that held diamonds and precious stones. And that isn't all! Mary gave the little old lady a seat of honor close to her throne.

The old lady enjoyed the music and she liked the singing by the angel choirs. She was anxious, however, to see Mary's gifts. Oh, there were so many packages, so many birthday gifts. Why, there was a present from everyone in heaven.

Now Mary didn't try to open all the presents right away, but there was one gift that Mary did open. It was a golden box that had been carried by four angels and placed at Mary's feet. No one knew what was in the box and all the angels wondered. I suppose you, too, are wondering what was in that box.

When the Blessed Virgin opened the box, she smiled. Then she closed the box and smiled again. Mary knew that all her friends in heaven were wondering what was in the box. So, she raised her hand and the music stopped. For a moment there was silence in heaven. Then Mary began to speak.

"A little old lady," said Mary, "has just come into heaven. This woman has brought a most beautiful gift, a box of Hail Marys. Every morning and night for seventy years, this woman has said three Hail Marys and all the Hail Marys are in this box. While on earth, this woman proved that she loved me. Now she has a place of honor in heaven."

The little old lady was certainly pleased with her first day in heaven. Yes, Mary's words were true. The woman had loved Mary on earth. Now she would be close to Mary forever.

I wish that you boys and girls would take that little old lady's story and make it your story. You, too, should love the Blessed Virgin Mary and you should pray to Mary every day. Remember, Mary is your mother and every child should love his mother. You should not only tell Mary that you love her, but you should show Mary that you love her. Show Mary that you love her by keeping away from sin because Mary hates sin! Show Mary that you love her by praying to her every single day!

Let me make a suggestion! Why don't you do what the little old lady did? Say three Hail Marys to the Blessed Virgin every morning and night! I know several people who do that, and they ask Mary to watch over them. They ask Mary to keep them from sin. They ask her to help them save their souls. It doesn't take much time to say three Hail Marys, but those three Hail Marys will tell the Blessed Virgin that you love her. Those three Hail Marys may help you to get into heaven. You know, Mary takes care of her friends. If you say those three Hail Marys every morning and night, Mary will take care of you. Now don't wait until tomorrow! Start today and say those Hail Marys every day!

You may not go to heaven on Mary's birthday, but when you do go, I hope Mary will be as anxious to see you as she was to see the little old lady. Mary will be waiting for you in heaven if you send ahead a box of Hail Marys.

11. Two Bags of Peanuts

THE OTHER AFTERNOON I drove to Webster Park. I go there every year during the month of October. At this time of the year, it's always quiet and peaceful in the park, and it's a grand place to spend an hour.

First of all, I parked my car and went for a short walk. Then, I bought two bags of peanuts. Now don't get the idea that I bought the peanuts for myself! Oh, no! I bought the peanuts for — well, you'll never guess.

I found a bench and sat down to rest. I was all alone, that is, I was alone for a short time. Then I had company. A couple of squirrels played in the grass before me, and, little by little, they came closer and closer. When the squirrels were a few feet away from me, they sat down and watched me.

"Say, Father," they seemed to ask, "haven't you got anything good for us?"

I certainly did have something good for my two little friends. Didn't I have two bags of peanuts? Well, I opened one of the bags and threw some peanuts to the squirrels. Then, what happened? Squirrels came running from all directions. Little gray squirrels and big gray squirrels, mama squirrels and papa squirrels, long-tailed squirrels and short-tailed squirrels, young squirrels and old squirrels, and they all stopped in front of me. What did the squirrels want? The squirrels wanted peanuts.

For a few minutes, I had a lot of fun. Every time I threw some peanuts to the squirrels, there was a wild scramble. Those squirrels certainly did like peanuts. But do you know what I noticed? The squirrels looked carefully at each peanut and they ate only the peanuts with holes or cracks. Whenever a squirrel found a peanut without holes or cracks, he kept that peanut and hurried away to hide it. Each squirrel had his own hiding place. When a squirrel hid his peanut, he came back for more.

Finally, my peanuts were gone. The bags were empty and the squirrels seemed very sad. They watched me for a long time, but I had no more peanuts. The fun was over, and I'm sure that the squirrels were disappointed.

Now, I think that those squirrels were very wise. They knew that the peanuts with holes or cracks would not keep. So, they ate them. But the squirrels stored away the good peanuts, the peanuts with no holes nor cracks. They knew the good peanuts would keep. During the winter, you know, squirrels don't have many chances to collect food. So, squirrels have to store away food enough to last them all winter.

That's why my little friends in the park hid their good peanuts. They were looking ahead. They were thinking about the long winter. The squirrels were storing up for the future.

Don't you think that you boys and girls can learn a very good lesson from the squirrels in the park? I think you can. Every time you do something good, you are storing up for the future. You know, God pays you for being good. God pays you for doing good. Every prayer you say, every Mass you hear, every Communion you receive, stores up grace for you. Every time you obey, every time you are honest, every time you speak the truth, you store up grace for your soul.

After you die, children, you will have no more chances to earn grace for your soul. You must earn grace now. Each day the squirrels in the park prepare for winter, and each day you must prepare for heaven. You can't afford to lose any time. Don't get the idea that you are going to live for a long time, and that you will have plenty of time to earn grace for your soul! You don't know how much time God will give you to save your soul. So, don't let a day go by without doing something good! Earn grace now and store it away for the future!

Wise squirrels look out for the future, and wise boys and girls look out for the future, too. You want to go to heaven. Well, now is the time to prepare for heaven. Now is the time to store up grace. Make every day count and let every day bring you closer to Christ and your home in heaven. Store up grace every day, and don't forget the lesson I learned while feeding squirrels two bags of peanuts!

12. The Penny Man

DURING THE PAST TWENTY YEARS, a Cleveland man has been a happy miser. During all that time this man has never spent a cent. That's right! During the past twenty years, this Cleveland man has never spent a penny.

Most misers, you know, are very unhappy. They think only about money — how they can make more money — how they can save more money. Then, too, misers are always worrying about their money, because they are afraid they are going to lose it. That's why most misers are unhappy. But this Cleveland man is a different kind of miser. He's a happy miser and he never spends a cent.

This man saves every penny he gets. When he goes to the store, when he buys gasoline, when he goes to the movies, he never spends the pennies he receives in change. He saves them. Of course, the man spends nickels, dimes, quarters, and dollar bills. He buys whatever he needs, but he never uses pennies. What does the man do with his pennies?

Well, this man has a large iron bank and he puts every penny he gets into the bank. Now, the man doesn't save those pennies for himself. Oh, no! The man saves the pennies for some of his little friends.

Once a year, the poor children of Cleveland have a picnic. The day before the picnic, the man who saves pennies, opens his iron bank and finds hundreds of pennies that he has saved during the year. The next day the man goes to the children's picnic and he carries his pennies in a wooden box.

When the children see their friend, they shout and yell: "Here comes the Penny Man! Here comes the Penny Man!" Then the children run and crowd about the smiling miser with his famous box of pennies.

The man takes the cover off his box and throws pennies in all directions. Of course, there is a wild scramble. The children shout and laugh as they try to catch the pennies and pick them off the ground. The penny scramble lasts for some time, until the box is empty, and by that time, every boy and girl has a good number of precious pennies.

Each year the children watch for the Penny Man. They know that he will always come to their picnic. They know, too, that the Penny Man will always have plenty of pennies for all of them. Never once has the Penny Man disappointed the children. He is always on the job making children happy, and making himself happy, too, with his box of pennies.

Children, do you know that the Penny Man acts

very much like God? Oh, I don't mean that God saves pennies and throws them away to little boys and girls. But I do mean that God has saved a lot of grace for each one of you. When God died on the Cross on that first Good Friday, He did something good. In fact, God's death on the Cross was the greatest thing that ever happened. Now, God should have received a great amount of grace for dying on the Cross, but God didn't need that grace. God could get into heaven without that grace. So what did God do? God saved that grace that He earned by dying on the Cross and He saved that grace for you. Any time you want some of that grace you can have it. You can have that grace by receiving the Sacraments.

God gives you grace through the Sacraments. Every time you receive one of the Sacraments, you receive grace in your soul. You don't have to wait a whole year to receive some of God's grace. Oh, no! If you receive Holy Communion every day, you receive some of God's grace every day. If you go to confession once a week, you receive grace once a week. Yes, every time you receive one of the Sacraments, you receive grace. God made the seven Sacraments to help you obtain grace.

Boys and girls, you need grace for your soul, and you can never have too much grace. God's grace will buy your way into heaven. That's why you should try to receive as much grace as possible. That's why you should go to confession and receive Holy Communion often. If you receive these Sacraments often, you will find it easy to get to heaven.

The children at the picnic try hard to get the Penny Man's pennies. You should try hard to get God's grace by receiving the Sacraments often.

13. Thirty-Five Cakes

EVERY BOY AND GIRL likes a picnic. A picnic means lots of fun. It's fun to go to a park and be outdoors. It's fun to swim, run races, and play games. But I think the best part of any picnic is the lunch. Children always get very hungry at picnics, and the lunch is a very important part of every picnic.

Last June the sixth grade of a certain school had a picnic. Before the picnic, the boys and girls had quite a few meetings and made their plans. They planned their games for the great event and decided what they would do when they went to the park.

"What about the lunch?" asked one little fellow at one of the meetings.

That was an important question and it brought all kinds of answers. Some children wanted pickles, and others wanted olives. Some wanted ham sandwiches, and others wanted cheese. One wanted watermelon, and another wanted pie. It seemed as though each child wanted something different. So, the children decided that each child should bring something to eat, whatever he wished, and then the food would be placed on a table and shared by all. Each child went home and told his mother that he had to bring some food for the picnic, and each child left it to his mother to decide just what that would be.

The sixth graders had a grand day for their picnic. The thirty-five boys and girls left school about ten o'clock in the morning, and rode by bus to the park. Each child carried a cardboard box or a basket that had been carefully packed by his mother. The children, judging the sizes of the different packages, felt pretty sure that they would have plenty to eat. At the park the boys had a ball game and it was certainly exciting. Then they had races for boys and others for girls. Some of the children went for a swim. A couple of boys even went fishing.

The children had a fine time at their picnic, and by one o'clock, they were all very hungry. The children sang songs while the Sisters opened the lunch boxes and baskets. No one noticed that the Sisters looked worried as they went about their work. The Sisters opened box after box and basket after basket. Finally, they finished, and one of the Sisters threw up her hands.

"What's the matter, Sister?" called out Freddie Carpenter. "Is there something wrong?"

Sister Helen Roberta was almost in tears. She nodded her head. There *was* something wrong. What do you think? Each child had brought food for the picnic but there were no pickles, no olives, no ham sandwiches, no cheese sandwiches, no sandwiches of any kind. There were no potato chips, no baked beans, no salad, no bread, no fruit. Well, I suppose you are wondering what the children did bring. Believe it or not, each child brought the same thing for the picnic. Each child brought a cake. In all, there were thirty-five cakes.

Thirty-five cakes! Chocolate, coconut, banana, and vanilla cakes! Plain cakes, frosted cakes, and cakes with nuts on them! Why, the picnic table looked like a bakery. Cakes! Cakes! Cakes! Thirty-five of them! That's all there was to eat. Thirty-five cakes for a picnic!

What did the children do? Well, there was only one thing that the children could do and they did it. They ate cake. They ate all kinds of cake. Even the Sisters ate cake and they pretended to like it. Cake and cake alone certainly wasn't the right food for a picnic lunch, but what else could the children and Sisters do? They just had to eat cake.

Now every boy and girl likes cake, but too much cake is not good. I don't have to tell you that there were a good many stomach aches at the picnic that afternoon. There were too many stomach aches, because there were too many cakes.

Sister Helen Roberta should have told each child just what to bring for the picnic. She should have told Peter to bring a cake. She should have told Mary to bring sandwiches. She should have asked Margaret to bring some salad, and Henry should have brought the pickles. If Sister Helen Roberta had done that, then the children would have had a grand picnic lunch, and there would have been fewer stomach aches.

Whether you get up a picnic lunch, have a Scout meeting, or play a game of ball, it's the way you do it that counts. There must be someone in charge and then things will run smoothly.

There is order in the Catholic Church because there is someone in charge. The Pope is in charge of the Church and he rules the Church for Christ. When Jesus was on earth, He taught certain things and pointed out certain things that people must do in order to get to heaven, and Jesus wants the people who live here now to know just what He taught. So, Jesus has placed the Pope in charge of the Church, and the Pope teaches the people what Jesus taught.

Of course, the Pope has helpers. He has bishops and priests under him and they help the Pope to teach. The bishops and priests can't teach just anything they wish; they must teach what Jesus taught and the Pope makes sure that the bishops and priests teach correctly. The Pope takes Christ's place in the Church, and because the Pope is in charge, everything in the Church runs smoothly and there are no mistakes.

The sixth-grade picnic was a failure because there was no one in charge of the lunch. There is always someone in charge of the Catholic Church. The Pope is in charge and he rules and guides the Catholic

Church for Christ. The Pope is our leader, our guide. He shows us the way to heaven. If we follow the Pope's directions, we will make no mistakes, and we will save our souls.

14. *Chippy*

EDDIE COOPER wanted a pet for his son, Teddy, who was seven months old. So, Eddie decided to buy a dog. He looked at all kinds of dogs, and finally, one day he bought a small puppy. Eddie named the dog, "Chippy."

Now, I don't have to tell you that little Teddy Cooper and Chippy became very good friends. The dog and the boy were always together. During the day they played together, and at night the dog slept under the little boy's bed. When Teddy was old enough to walk, Chippy was always by his side. They were two good friends who grew up together, two friends who loved each other.

Chippy always took pretty good care of his little friend. When Chippy thought Teddy was hungry, he brought him an apple. When the boy lost one of his toys, Chippy always found it for him. When it was time to get ready for bed, Chippy found the boy's slippers and held them in his mouth. These things happened day after day. They were the dog's way of showing his friend that he loved him.

Of course, Teddy was very good to the dog, too.

He was always kind. When he played with the dog, he was never rough, and he never did anything to hurt his pet in any way. Teddy petted the dog often, and he did his very best to make the dog happy.

For six long years Teddy Cooper and Chippy were friends. Then something terrible happened. Teddy Cooper became very sick. For seven weeks Teddy suffered night and day. The doctors and nurses tried hard to help the little boy, but God wanted Teddy in heaven, and God had His way. So, the dog was left behind.

Chippy was a sad dog without Teddy. For three days the dog stayed under the boy's bed and wouldn't eat. Chippy had lost his best friend, and he found it hard to live without him. Then, the dog began to act very strangely. Each morning the dog disappeared, but he always came back at night. No one knew where the dog went. No one knew where the dog spent his time.

One day Mrs. Cooper discovered that some of Teddy's toys and pieces of clothing were missing. She looked all over the house, but couldn't find them. Finally, she spoke to one of the neighbors. And what do you think? The neighbor told Mrs. Cooper that she had seen Chippy going down the street with a slipper in his mouth. So, the next morning Mrs. Cooper watched the dog, and sure enough, she saw Chippy leave the house with a cap in his mouth.

There was only one thing for Mrs. Cooper to do. She followed the dog, and where do you think the dog led her? Chippy led her to Teddy's grave. And was Mrs. Cooper surprised? There on the grave the woman found several toys, a rubber, a slipper, and two socks. The dog had carried all these things to the boy's grave.

Chippy thought his friend needed his toys and clothing. Even though Teddy was dead, Chippy didn't forget his friend. The dog was faithful to his friend and tried to help him. But the grave stopped the kind little animal.

When our friends die, children, the grave doesn't stop us. Oh, no! When our friends die, we can still help them. We can help them by our prayers.

What about your friends who have died? Have you forgotten them? Do you ever pray for your friends who have passed away? Your friends may be suffering in purgatory and they may need your prayers. The souls in purgatory cannot pray for themselves, but you can pray for them. You can help them in their sufferings. You can shorten their time in purgatory.

The dog in our story thought that he was helping his little friend, but really, he wasn't helping him. That isn't the way it is with us. We really can help our dead. If you knew someone who was suffering, wouldn't you help him? Certainly, you would. Well, the souls in purgatory are suffering and they are crying out to you for help. They want your prayers, lots of prayers, because your prayers will send them to God.

Boys and girls, there are many souls in purgatory

who have no one to pray for them. They suffer and suffer and suffer. Perhaps a few prayers from you will get one of those souls into heaven. Why don't you try to get that soul into heaven today? Say some prayers for the Poor Souls during Mass this morning! Remember them in your prayers tonight! Remember the Poor Souls every day!

Prayer is a wonderful thing. Prayer does wonderful things for people who live on earth, and it helps the dead, too. So, get busy with your prayers! Pray for your own dead first! Then pray for the Poor Souls in purgatory! The Poor Souls need your help. They need your prayers.

15. Marty's First Mass

MARTY LEE, a boy about ten, lived in a small town just outside New York City. Marty was not an altar boy, but he was studying to be an altar boy. Twice a week he went to Father Howard's class to learn how to serve at the altar, and every night the boy studied the prayers of the Mass. Marty was very anxious to be an altar boy, and he could hardly wait for the day when he would serve his first Mass.

Easter Sunday came and Marty went with his father and mother to the ten o'clock Mass. Now Marty didn't sit in the pew with his parents. Oh, no! The little fellow sat in one of the first pews with the other children. He liked to sit up in the front; there he could watch the boys serving at the altar.

The church bell rang at ten o'clock, but Mass didn't begin at once. There was a wait of several minutes and Marty wondered why Father Howard didn't begin the Mass. Finally, the door opened and Father Howard walked out alone. The priest didn't go to the altar as usual but, instead, he turned toward the people.

"This is Easter Sunday," the priest said, "and no boy has come to serve my Mass. Is there anyone in the church who can serve my Mass?"

Father Howard waited and no one offered to serve the Mass. Then the priest looked down at the children in the front pews and, sure enough, he saw Marty Lee.

"Marty," said the priest softly, "come and serve my Mass!"

Marty's heart jumped, and his face turned white. He had never served Mass before and now Father Howard wanted him to serve on Easter Sunday. The little fellow left his pew and hurried into the vestry where Father Howard helped him to dress.

"Now don't be nervous, Marty!" smiled the priest as he patted the boy on the shoulder and both started for the altar.

The Mass began, and little Marty felt that every eye in the church was on him. Was he nervous? Certainly, he was nervous! He was so nervous that he was scared and afraid. The little fellow stumbled through the Latin prayers as best he could, and he tried to remember everything that Father Howard had taught him. When Marty changed the book, he tripped and almost fell, but I guess his Guardian Angel saved him. Only once did the little fellow make a mistake. He rang the bell at the wrong time. Otherwise, he did very well. You can bet that Marty was mighty happy when Mass was over and he was back in the vestry.

"Marty, you did very well," said Father Howard with a smile.

"Gee, but I was awful nervous," answered the boy. "Maybe, I'll do better the next time."

Marty changed his clothes, and he was about to leave for home when the priest handed him a white box and an envelope.

"I had these for my regular altar boy," the priest said to Marty, "but you certainly deserve them."

The boy thanked the priest, and, on his way home, Marty opened the white box, and he found in it a large chocolate egg. Now I suppose you are wondering what the boy found in the envelope. Well, when Marty opened the envelope, he could hardly believe his eyes. He looked a second time to be sure. Yes, he had made no mistake. Marty found a five-dollar bill in the envelope and a beautiful Easter card. Father Howard had written on the card these words: "Happy Easter to a boy who served well!"

Did Marty Lee have a happy Easter? Well, he certainly did have a happy Easter. Marty was the happiest boy in that town, happy because he had served his first Mass, and he had served it alone. Not only had Marty served his first Mass, but Father Howard had rewarded him. He received a large chocolate egg and a five-dollar bill because he served well.

Father Howard, you know, isn't the only one who gives a reward for serving well. Almighty God does the same thing. God rewards everyone who serves

Him well, and God's reward is the best reward of all. God's reward is heaven.

There is only one thing that God asks you to do. He asks you to serve Him well. How do you serve God well? By keeping His laws, by saying your prayers, by going to Mass on Sunday, by receiving the Sacraments! God wants you to have lots of fun during your life, but He doesn't want you to forget Him. He wants you to love Him and He wants you to serve Him. Don't forget that God has promised a reward to those who serve Him well, and that reward is heaven. You can't buy your way into heaven. You must earn your way into heaven. You must serve God not once in a while, but every single day. If you are faithful to God in all things, if you serve Him well, you're bound to go to heaven.

Some day, you will stand before God, and God will judge you for every thought, word, and action of your whole life. I hope, that when you stand before God, He will smile on you and will reward you with a place in heaven. Yes, heaven is God's reward for boys and girls who serve well.

16. The Saturday Morning Special

I SUPPOSE many of you boys and girls have a pet. I know that some of you have a dog, and some have a cat. Maybe you have a canary bird that sings. Well, in my house we have no pets. I used to have a dog, but I don't have a dog now. I don't have a cat, and I don't have a canary bird. However, I do have a pet that visits my house every day.

Several months ago, a strange cat came up on my side porch and began to cry. My housekeeper felt sorry for the cat, and she gave the cat some milk. The cat drank the milk and then went away.

The next morning the cat came back, and, once again, the housekeeper gave him some milk. After the cat drank the milk, he went away. Now don't get the idea that that was the last time we saw that cat. No, sir! Every morning the cat came to the porch, and every morning the housekeeper fed him. After several days, we found out where the cat lived. Why, the cat lived away down on the end of the street, and his name was Tiger.

For several months now, Tiger has been coming

to our house every morning for breakfast, and his usual breakfast is a dish of milk. But here's something that will make you smile. We always have fish on Friday and, most of the time, there is some fish left. So, when Tiger comes on Saturday morning, he finds a special treat waiting for him. He finds not only milk, but he finds fish, too. And Tiger certainly likes fish. But do you know what Tiger does on Saturday mornings? First of all, he drinks his milk. Then the cat disappears. Where does he go? Well, you'll be surprised.

Tiger has a friend down the street and Tiger's friend likes fish, too. So, every Saturday morning, Tiger goes and calls his friend. Then, the two cats hurry to my side porch, and they eat fish together.

Now can't you see why I like Tiger? Yes, Tiger is an unusual cat. He's not selfish. He likes fish, but he likes to share his fish with his friend. Oh, I think Tiger can teach you boys and girls a very good lesson.

Boys and girls, we all like people who are generous and kind, and you should be generous and kind. That doesn't mean that you have to give away everything you own. Oh, no! But it does mean that you should share with others. You should let other children play with your toys, and you should let them play in your games. You should be generous with your apples and give others some of your candy. You should teach children how to skate or ride a bicycle. You should help your friends with their work. Oh, there are so many ways by which you can share with others, so many ways by which you can help others, so many ways by which you can be generous and kind.

Remember, children, there are many boys and girls who don't have as much as you have. If you will share your things with others, you'll feel a lot better inside. You'll not only make others happy, but you'll make yourself happy, too. If you will share with your friends, your friends will share with you. Above all, be sure to share with your brothers and sisters! You love them more than anyone else in this world. If you will share with your family, you'll have a happy home.

You don't like anyone who is selfish. You don't like a stingy person. You don't want to play with a stingy person, or a selfish person. You keep away from him. Isn't that true? Certainly, it is! Well, if you are stingy and selfish, other boys and girls won't like you. They'll keep away from you, and you don't want that to happen.

You children are trying to walk in the footsteps of Jesus. Well, Jesus was always kind. He was kind to everybody. He was kind even to those who hated Him. Jesus was always trying to help others. If you will be kind to others, you'll be doing just what Jesus did, and Jesus will bless you for it. The best way to be kind is to share with your friends. Don't be thinking about yourself all the time! Think about others, and share!

17. The Boy Who Saved Christmas

EDDIE MOORE believed in Christmas. He knew that Christmas was the birthday of Jesus, and he also knew that Santa Claus visited the homes of children on Christmas Eve and left presents. Now Eddie's mother was too poor to buy presents for the boy, but the little fellow was sure that Santa Claus would take care of everything. He wanted Santa to bring him a sled, a drum, a red auto, and a box of candy. Eddie felt that those four things would make him very happy.

The little boy went to bed early on Christmas Eve. Before he went to bed, he hung his stocking from a shelf in the kitchen. Then he said his prayers, and soon the boy was sound asleep. All through that long night Eddie dreamed about sleds and drums and red autos and boxes of candy.

The next morning Eddie awoke very early. He jumped out of bed and ran to the kitchen. There the boy found his stocking just as he had left it the night before, and the stocking was empty. There was no sled, no drum, no red auto, no box of candy. Eddie was heartbroken, and how he cried! The boy was puzzled. He couldn't understand why Santa Claus had forgotten him. Without a doubt, Eddie Moore was the saddest boy in this whole, whole world.

After Mass Eddie met some of his friends. Of course, they all talked about their presents. Eddie listened, but said nothing. He felt worse then than when he found the empty stocking. While they were talking, one of the boys said that Santa Claus would be at the Firemen's Club that night, and that he would have more toys and presents.

Eddie's eyes sparkled and his heart beat faster. Eddie wanted to go to the Firemen's Club. He wanted to see Santa Claus. Perhaps, this time Santa would have something for him.

The Firemen's Club was near Eddie's home and the boy's mother agreed to let him go to the Christmas party. That was good news for Eddie, and the boy lived in hope through that long Christmas afternoon. Surely, he felt, Santa Claus will not forget me again.

That night Eddie went to the Firemen's Club with a shining face, and his hair well combed and brushed. His heart was light and happy. The boy entered the Club and sat alone. He listened to the music and singing, but kept his eyes fixed on the tall Christmas tree that stood in the center of the large stage.

After some time, sleigh bells began to ring. There

was silence in the hall, and then cheers as Santa Claus walked across the stage. He carried a large bag filled with toys and presents.

Little Eddie stood up and his heart pounded within him. He heard Santa call out the names of boys and girls. Now there was one thing that Eddie didn't know. He didn't know that the boys and girls called, were all children whose fathers were firemen. Eddie saw Santa Claus give skates to Tommy, a doll to Helen, a football to Johnny, a drum to Ted. Some boys and girls received more than one present. In fact, some received three or four presents, and finally, Santa's big bag was empty.

Eddie Moore was the only boy in the hall whose name was not called. He was the only boy in the hall without a present. Twice in the same day, Eddie had been forgotten, and for the second time Santa Claus had broken the little boy's heart. Eddie cried and sobbed and started for the door.

As Eddie walked down the steps, a strange boy touched him on the shoulder. "You haven't any present," said the stranger, "and I have four. Here, take this!" and he handed Eddie a package.

Eddie was so excited that he couldn't speak. Quickly, he tore off the paper that covered a box of candy. When Eddie saw the box, he could hardly believe his eyes. Candy was one of the things he wanted. Eddie turned to thank his friend, but the strange boy was gone.

That night when Eddie knelt down to pray, he

said a prayer for a strange boy whose name he didn't know. Then Eddie jumped into bed and he was very happy. But there was another boy who was happy, too, the strange boy who saved Christmas for Eddie Moore.

Children, I think you understand very well the lesson of this story. Be kind and generous to others! If you want to be happy, just do a good deed for someone. You don't have to wait until Christmas to do that good deed, either. You can do a good deed today. Perhaps your good deed will save this day for some brokenhearted child, just as the kind act of a strange boy saved Christmas for little Eddie Moore.

18. The Man in the Blue Overalls

BOB COLE'S father was not a rich man. He was a carpenter and a hard worker, a man who made many sacrifices for his son. The father wanted his boy to have a good education and that's why he sent Bob to college.

Now, it takes lots of money to send a boy to college, and Bob's father did without a good many things for the sake of his son. Bob's father never owned an automobile. He never bought many clothes. He never took a vacation. The father went without all those things in order to pay Bob's way through college.

Bob was grateful, and he knew that his father was suffering for him. So, while he was in college, Bob worked hard at his studies and he graduated with honors. After college, Bob went to work in a bank. At first, of course, Bob didn't get much pay for his work in the bank, but every week he gave some of his money to his father. The son tried to show his father that he was grateful. Bob tried to pay back all that his father had given to him.

Bob Cole worked hard in the bank and he rose higher and higher. Finally, Bob became vice-president of the bank. Now, the vice-president of a bank is a mighty important person, but Bob Cole didn't change. No, sir! Bob was always good to his father. Even though his father was only a carpenter and didn't wear fine clothes, Bob was proud of him.

Well, one day the young men of the town had a luncheon to honor their fathers. Each son invited his father to lunch and all the important people of the town were present. There were doctors, lawyers, teachers, storekeepers, and businessmen at the luncheon, and everyone was dressed in his best clothes. Every young man at the luncheon was proud of his father, and every father was proud of his son. Some of the men wondered why Bob Cole and his father were not at the luncheon. Was the carpenter's son ashamed of his father?

No, boys and girls, Bob Cole was not ashamed of his father. While the men were eating lunch, the door opened and Bob Cole and his father entered the room. Bob's father wore blue overalls that were dirty and patched. A blue handkerchief stuck out of his pocket. His hands were dirty and his hair was mussed.

Bob and his father did not sit down at a table. Instead, they stood in the center of the large room and Bob raised his hand. Immediately there was silence, and every man looked at Bob Cole and the man in the blue overalls.

"Pardon me, gentlemen!" spoke out Bob in a clear voice. "I am sorry for interrupting your party. We can't stay for lunch because my father has to get back to work. I want you to meet my dad, Peter Cole, the man who worked so hard to send me to college. He is a carpenter, a good carpenter, and I'm mighty proud of him."

That's all Bob said. He and his father turned to leave, and every man in that room clapped and cheered.

Bob Cole wasn't ashamed of his father. Even though his father didn't have fine clothes, even though his father wore blue overalls, Bob Cole felt that his father was the best father of all. Bob didn't forget what his father had done for him. He was proud of his father and he wanted everyone to know it. That day Bob taught those men at the luncheon a lesson. I hope that you'll learn the same lesson this morning.

Almighty God has given each of you children a father and a mother. Your parents work hard for you. They give you a home, clothes, and food; they send you to school. All these things cost lots of money. Your parents go without things because they want you to have the best. They do all these things because they love you, and because they are mighty proud of you.

What do your parents ask in return? They don't

want money from you. Oh, no! But they do want your love. They want you to obey them. They want you to respect them. You will never have to do as much for your parents as they have done for you. Remember, your parents take God's place, and when they ask you to do something, it is just the same as though God asked you to do it. When you disobey your parents, you disobey God.

Your parents may not wear fine clothes because they have spent their money for fine clothes for you. Bob Cole's father wore dirty overalls and Bob was proud of him. That's the way you should feel about your father and mother. Never mind about your parents' clothes because their hearts are right! Your parents love you, and you should love them. You should obey your parents. You should respect them.

Children, don't ever be ashamed of your parents! Remember, God gave you the best father and the best mother in this world. Respect your parents! Obey them, and love them! Like Bob Cole, you have every reason to be mighty proud of your father and your mother.

19. The Only Key

TOMMY WILLIAMS was a Boy Scout. Tommy liked scouting and he learned many useful and interesting things. He liked the Scout meetings and he liked to march in parades. Every summer, too, the Scouts went to camp and that's what Tommy liked best. He liked to live in the open, hike through the woods, cook his own meals, and sleep in a tent.

At one of the September meetings, the Scoutmaster told the boys that he was going to take them to Philadelphia during the Easter vacation. When the boys heard that, they clapped and cheered. That was certainly good news. There was one thing, however, that the boys would have to do. They would have to help raise the money for the trip.

Tommy and his friends got busy. For several months they worked on all kinds of plans to raise money. The boys cut grass, shoveled snow, and did odd jobs. They sold candy and gum to their schoolmates. They had a show in the school hall and a pet show in Tommy's yard. The boys worked hard, and they saved the money they made for the Easter trip. The boys were certainly excited and they thought Easter week would never come.

Well, Easter week did come and the boys went to Philadelphia. Oh, they had a wonderful time! They toured the city, visited the parks, and saw many interesting things. But the most interesting place of all was Independence Hall. The boys could hardly believe that the building was two hundred years old.

Tommy Williams had a special interest in Independence Hall because he had studied about it in school. This was the place where the Declaration of Independence was signed. Here, too, the Constitution was adopted, and in this building George Washington received the command of the Continental Army. Independence Hall was a very important place, especially, to Tommy Williams.

A guide showed the boys through the various rooms of Independence Hall and explained everything. The guide showed the boys the table where the Declaration of Independence was signed. He showed them the silver inkstand used by the men who signed the Declaration. Finally, the guide showed them the Liberty Bell that rang out for the first time in 1776.

Tommy Williams was thrilled at everything he saw. It was a great day in Tommy's life, a day that he would never forget.

When the guide had shown the boys everything, he held up a key. "This key," said the man, "is the only key in the world that will open the door of Independence Hall."

The boys admired the key and then Tommy Williams surprised everybody. "I'll bet I can open the door of Independence Hall," said Tommy as he pulled a large key from his pocket.

The guide smiled and he didn't argue. "All right, young fellow," said the guide, "if you think you can open the door, we'll give you a chance."

Tommy stepped outside and the guide locked the door from the inside. What happened? Everyone was surprised when Tommy unlocked the door in a few seconds and walked into the room. Tommy's key was a skeleton key, or a master key, a special key that will open any door.

Would you like to have a special key that will open the gates of heaven for you? Oh, I suppose you think that Saint Peter has the only key to the gates of heaven. Well, Saint Peter does have a key to the gates of heaven, but you can have a key, too. Yes, you can! Your key to heaven is your soul when it is in the state of grace.

Some day each one of you will die. If you die with one mortal sin on your soul, you won't be able to get into heaven. If you die in the state of grace, and that means that you have no mortal sins on your soul, you will certainly get into heaven. Of course, if you have some small sins on your soul, you will have to spend some time in Purgatory. But, after Purgatory, you will go to heaven.

How does a boy or girl get into the state of grace? By going to confession! Confession takes away every mortal sin, and after confession, you are in the state of grace. If you never commit another mortal sin, you remain in the state of grace. Why, you can stay in the state of grace for years and years. You can live in the state of grace forever. Thousands and thousands of people never commit a mortal sin. They are living in the state of grace.

There is only one thing that will keep you out of heaven, and that is mortal sin. Don't take any chances! If you should fall into mortal sin, go to confession quickly! Always be in the state of grace! The state of grace is your key to heaven.

20. The City Without Walls

HUNDREDS OF YEARS AGO the cities of old Greece had high walls built around them. The walls were made of stone, and there were iron gates at the various roads that led into the city. Soldiers guarded the walls and gates of the cities at all times.

I suppose you are wondering why walls were built around the cities of Greece. The people built walls around their cities to protect themselves from their enemies. In those days there were many wars, and in time of war the walls made it hard for enemies to enter the cities. The walls blocked the enemies every time. So, a very high wall around a city was always very important.

Here's something that may surprise you. Do you know that there was one city in Greece that had no walls around it? Yes, that's true! The city of Sparta had no walls around it. The city of Sparta had no gates, no soldiers guarding the city. Sparta stood alone, the only city in Greece without walls.

Now, the King of Sparta was a very fine king. He was neither proud nor hard, but he was kind and generous, and his people loved him. The King was good to his people and he tried to be their friend. He tried, too, to be friendly with his neighbors. So, what do you think the King did? One day the King of Sparta invited the kings of neighboring cities to come and visit him.

Of course, when the people of Sparta heard that strange kings were coming to their city, they prepared a grand welcome. Yes, there was a parade, a big parade with soldiers, flags, and music. As the kings rode through the city, the people of Sparta waved and cheered. The visiting kings were quite surprised at the welcome they received.

When the visiting kings reached the palace, the King of Sparta was very kind to his guests. He had prepared a grand feast, but just before the visiting kings sat down at table, one of the visitors asked a question.

"King of Sparta," he asked, "why do you have no walls to protect your city?"

The King of Sparta smiled. He waved his hand and led the visiting kings to a window.

The King pointed to thousands of his people who were gathered in the courtyard. "These are my walls," said the King of Sparta. "My people are my walls."

Yes, the people of Sparta were the walls of the city. The people of Sparta loved their King and every person in that city was a soldier. Every person was a soldier ready at any time to defend the city and protect the King, a soldier ready to fight for his

King, a soldier ready to die for his King. No wonder that the city of Sparta had no walls. Sparta needed no walls. The people were the walls of the city.

Boys and girls, this afternoon many of you will receive the Sacrament of Confirmation. You will receive the Holy Ghost. God will come to you and He will strengthen you in your faith. This afternoon, you will become members of Christ's army. This afternoon, you will become soldiers of Jesus Christ.

As a soldier you must be loyal to Christ, your King. You must obey Him and you must serve Him well. You must be ready at all times to protect Christ, to defend Christ from His enemies. You must be ready to fight for Christ — yes, die for Christ.

Like the King of Sparta, Christ has no walls. In the future you will be Christ's walls, and Christ will depend upon you to protect Him. When people talk about Christ, you must defend Him. When people break Christ's laws, you must correct them. By your life and your good example, you must show the world that you believe in Christ, that you love Christ, that you are one of Christ's soldiers.

Now don't get the idea that, just because you are going to be a soldier, you will have to be fighting all the time. The best way to be a soldier of Christ is to live well by saying your prayers, keeping God's laws, and receiving the Sacraments often. By doing these things you will prove to Christ that you are loyal to Him, that you love Him. Of course, there will be times when you will have to defend Christ. You won't have to defend Christ with your fists. Oh, no! Very often, a kind word or a good deed will protect Christ from His enemies.

Children, you know what is right. Don't be afraid to do right at all times! You know what Christ wants and what He expects you to do. At times, it may be hard, but a good soldier never runs away from his duty. It's an honor to be a soldier of Christ. Don't ever be a traitor! Be a good soldier at all times! Be loyal to Jesus Christ!

21. The Girl in the Shabby Dress

LITTLE ETHEL CLARK wanted to make her First Communion. Every day she studied her catechism and said her prayers, and very often the little girl visited Jesus in the church. Ethel longed for the day when she would receive Jesus for the first time.

You can imagine how excited Ethel was the day the priest called the names of the children for the First Communion class. Yes, Ethel's name was called, and she was so happy that she ran all the way home to tell the good news to her mother.

Ethel's mother, however, was not so happy. "You're only seven and you're too young to make your First Communion," said the mother to the little girl. "Besides, we haven't money enough to buy you new clothes. No, Ethel, you can't make your First Communion this year."

Ethel's heart was broken. She couldn't make her First Communion! Oh, how the little girl cried! But tears wouldn't make the mother change her mind. She was determined that Ethel would not make her First Communion.

Of course, Ethel was disappointed, and Jesus was disappointed, too. Jesus wanted to come to Ethel, but the girl's mother said that Jesus would have to wait.

Well, Ethel didn't give up. Oh, no! She prayed and prayed and prayed. And Ethel did something more. Every afternoon she went to the First Communion class. Even though Ethel wasn't going to make her First Communion, the girl wanted to learn all about Jesus.

Now, Ethel never told the priest or the Sisters that her mother didn't want her to make her First Communion. So, the day before First Communion day, when the children went to confession, Ethel went to confession, too. Of course, after confession the girl was very happy, but she knew that the next day she would be very sad. All the other little girls would wear white dresses and white veils, but Ethel would have no white dress, no white veil. All the other children in the class would receive Jesus for the first time — they would make their First Communion — but Ethel would have to wait. She would have to wait until she was older. Then, maybe, her parents could buy her a white dress.

The next morning Saint Clement's Church was crowded with parents and friends who came to see the children make their First Communion. The First Communion class sat in the center aisle, the boys wearing white shirts and white ties, the girls wearing white dresses and white veils. I said that the First Communion class sat in the center aisle.

Yes, that's right! The children were all there, all except one little girl, and that little girl was Ethel Clark. Ethel sat in the side aisle wearing a shabby blue dress and her sister's hat. Ethel tried to pray and she tried to forget about the children in the center aisle, but it was too hard. Ethel wanted Jesus. She wanted Jesus so much. Ethel wanted to make her First Communion.

Ethel watched the boys as they marched to the altar rail. She saw each one of them receive Jesus for the first time. Then she watched the girls. Rosemary Statt! Helen Connors! Judy Barker! Mary O'Grady! Susie Dale! Well, when Ethel saw Susie Dale kneeling at the rail, her heart pounded within her. Ethel should have been kneeling next to Susie Dale. When Susie Dale received Holy Communion, Ethel became so excited that she stood up and called out at the top of her voice: "I want little Jesus! I want Jesus, too!"

The priest was so surprised that he stopped for a moment. Then he motioned to Ethel to come up to the rail. And what do you think? Ethel Clark hurried up the aisle, knelt next to Susie Dale, and received Holy Communion. Yes, Ethel Clark made her First Communion in her shabby blue dress and her sister's hat.

Now I don't have to tell you that Ethel was happy that morning. Even though the girl didn't have a new dress, Jesus loved her just as much as the other children in that First Communion class. Ethel's soul was clean, and her heart was filled with love, and that's all that counted with Jesus. Why, I don't suppose that Jesus even noticed the shabby blue dress. He looked at the girl's soul and saw it was right. That's why Jesus made Ethel so happy.

Boys and girls, I wish that more of you were like Ethel Clark. You should want Jesus just as much as Ethel did. Jesus is God, you know, and He can do much for you. That's why you should want Him. That's why you should receive Him often in Holy Communion. Why, if you have no mortal sins on your soul, you can receive Jesus every day. I know you all love Jesus, but why don't you show your love by receiving Jesus often? Jesus wants you, and you should want Him. You need Jesus. You need His graces.

Children, you must save your own soul. No one else can save your soul for you. You must do it yourself. Every time you receive Holy Communion, you receive Jesus and you receive graces that help you save your soul. Don't neglect Jesus and don't neglect His graces! Receive Holy Communion often!

22. The Little Man in the Tree

IF JESUS WERE TO COME to our city tomorrow, what would you do? Oh, I think I know the answer. If Jesus were to come tomorrow, you would go to see Him and you would try to meet Him. Well, that's just what the people did when Jesus lived on this earth. Wherever Jesus went, large crowds turned out to see Him. The people wanted to hear Jesus speak. They wanted to see Him perform a miracle.

A short time before He died, Jesus went to the city of Jericho. Of course, that was a great day for the people of Jericho. They crowded the road and everyone tried to have a good place. Everyone wanted to see the great Jesus.

Now, that day in Jericho, there was one man who had a very hard time. That man was Zacheus and he was very short. Zacheus was so short that I suppose his friends called him "Shorty." Naturally, Zacheus wanted to see Jesus, and he tried very hard to get a good place. Well, every time Zacheus tried to push his way through the crowd, the people pushed him back. Time and time again, he tried to get to the front row, but every time the people blocked his way. Poor Zacheus! There he was, a little fellow, standing in the back row. He might just as well have stayed at home because he could see nothing. The tall people refused to give Zacheus a chance.

Zacheus was worried. Jesus would soon be coming. Jesus would soon pass down the road. Everyone would see Jesus, everyone except Zacheus, the little man in the back row.

All of a sudden, Zacheus had an idea and it was a good one. What do you think he did? Zacheus ran as fast as he could along the edge of the crowd and, finally, he came to a tree. Yes, you guessed it. Zacheus climbed up the tree and sat on one of the branches. Now he had a good place, the best place of all, and he could see everything. Now he would certainly see Jesus.

At last, Jesus came down the road. The people smiled and cheered, and many of them pointed to the man in the tree. Yes, Jesus saw Zacheus, all right, and He must have been pleased, because Jesus did something that surprised the crowd. Jesus stopped, looked at Zacheus, and spoke to him.

"Zacheus," said Christ, "hurry up and come down, for I must stay in your house today."

Well, it didn't take very long for Zacheus to get

out of that tree. The little man was so excited that he almost fell out of the tree, and, in a short time, Jesus and Zacheus walked down the road together.

That was a great day for the people of Jericho. They saw Jesus and they were very happy. But the happiest man in Jericho was Zacheus. He not only saw Jesus, but he had Jesus as a guest in his home. All of the people wanted Jesus in their homes, but Jesus honored only one man. Jesus honored Zacheus, the little man He found sitting in a tree.

Do you know, boys and girls, that Jesus wants to visit your home? Yes, Jesus wants to be a guest in your soul. Jesus wants to come to you and He wants to come often. Every time you receive Holy Communion, Jesus comes to you and He brings grace for your soul. Wouldn't it have been terrible, if Zacheus had refused to let Jesus come to his house? Yes, that would have been awful. Yet, that's just what you tell Jesus when you don't receive Him in Holy Communion. You tell Jesus that you don't want Him, that you don't need Him. Now I don't have to tell you that that's wrong. Jesus wants to come to you and many times you refuse to let Him come.

Zacheus had Jesus in his home for just one day. But you can do better than that. If you wish, you can have Jesus every day. At least, you should have Jesus with you every Sunday. You need Jesus and you need His graces. That's why you should receive Holy Communion often. So, make it a habit of receiving Holy Communion every Sunday! Start off every week in the right way by receiving Jesus in Holy Communion!

Children, Jesus is knocking on the door of your heart. He wants to come into your soul. Open that door and keep that door open! Let Jesus come to you often in Holy Communion!

23. The Girl Who Went Calling

LAST WEEK there was plenty of excitement in one of our near-by towns. What happened? Well, a little six-year-old girl caused all the excitement. Of course, little Elizabeth Brush didn't mean to do any harm but she certainly made her parents and friends suffer.

Last Tuesday, while Elizabeth's mother was preparing supper, the little girl went out into the yard to play. When supper was ready, Mrs. Brush called the girl, but the girl didn't answer. The mother went into the yard but Elizabeth wasn't there. The mother called and called but received no answer. Then the girl's mother and father hurried to the homes of neighbors, but no one had seen the little girl. Little Elizabeth Brush had disappeared.

You can imagine how worried the parents were and they thought some terrible thoughts. They wondered where Elizabeth had gone. Where was she? Why didn't the little girl come home?

Finally, the girl's father called the police and they promised to help. All the neighbors said they would help, too. So, it was decided that two persons would go down each street and stop at every house. In this way every house in the town would be visited in a short time. If Elizabeth were in someone's house, she would surely be found.

I might as well tell you now that the searchers visited every house in the town but no one had seen Elizabeth. That was sad news for the girl's parents. They cried and sobbed and prayed to God to help them.

While Mr. Brush was talking to friends outside his house, all of a sudden, he heard music. He heard organ music and the music was coming from the near-by church. The father knew that there were no services in the church, but he ran to the church as fast as he could. He hurried up the stairs where he found a man tuning and fixing the organ.

Mr. Brush didn't have a chance to speak before the man at the organ asked him a question.

"Are you looking for that little girl who is sitting down in the front seat?"

The father turned quickly and, sure enough, he saw little Elizabeth sitting in the front seat of the church. Mr. Brush hurried down the steps, ran up the aisle, and picked up the girl in his arms.

"Elizabeth," said the father excitedly, "we've been looking all over for you. We thought you were lost. What are you doing here?"

"I ain't been lost, Daddy," answered the little girl. "I heard the music and I came to talk to Jesus."

Little Elizabeth should have told her parents that she was going to the church. However, I think that all the worry and excitement must have made Jesus smile. You can be sure that Jesus was happy to see Elizabeth, because Jesus always likes to have little children visit Him.

Children, Jesus is here on our altar every day and He is here all through the night. He waits and waits and wishes that children would come and visit Him. The more often children come to the church, the better Jesus likes it. He knows that children who come are His friends. He knows that children come because they love Him.

How often do you visit a church? How often do you visit Jesus? Oh, there are so many times when you could stop to see Him. Most of you could stop every day. Yes, you could stop in the church on your way home from school. Of course, you come to church every Sunday, but Jesus wants to see you more often than once a week. When you visit Jesus, you don't have to stay in the church for a long time. If you stay for only a few minutes, Jesus will like it. Jesus knows that you are busy and that you like to play, but He does want you to give Him a little time.

There are so many things that you want for your family, for your friends, and for yourself. When you visit Jesus, ask Him for all those things! Thank Him, too, for being so good to you! Thank Him for your parents and friends! Thank Him for your health and for helping you with your work in school! Remember, Jesus will hear everything you say.

Children, don't neglect Jesus in the Blessed Sacrament! Visit Him often! Don't stay away from your best Friend!

24. The Tablet Without a Name

SEVERAL YEARS AGO I visited the United States Military Academy at West Point. The school at West Point, you know, is where young men are trained to be officers in the United States Army. I saw many interesting things at West Point. I saw the grounds and the buildings. I saw the young men at their games, and I saw them march and drill. It was a sight that I shall never forget.

I saw one thing at West Point that certainly made me think. The walls of one of the halls in this famous school are covered with tablets or plaques. The name of an American general is written on each one of the tablets. So, this hall is a hall of honor, a hall of fame, a hall where the name of every American general will live forever.

But what do you think? I found one tablet in that hall without a name. Yes, one tablet was blank. One tablet had no writing. I wondered about that blank tablet and thought it very strange. Finally, I spoke to my guide.

"Why is there no name on that one tablet?" I asked.

The guide waited for a moment before he spoke. "Father," he said, "that tablet belongs to Benedict Arnold, the traitor, the man who betrayed his country. That tablet has been left blank to show the great honor Benedict Arnold lost by not serving his country."

I think, children, that somewhere in heaven, Almighty God must have a special hall. There are plaques or tablets on the walls of that hall, too. Now what do you think is written on those tablets in heaven? The names of Christ's generals — the names of Sisters and priests who have been loyal to Jesus Christ. You will find written on the tablets in heaven the names of Saint Teresa, Saint Francis de Sales, the Little Flower, and thousands of other famous priests and nuns.

Every boy and girl who has been called by God to be a priest or nun has a tablet set aside in heaven. Are you one of these boys or girls? Is God calling you? Is God asking you to be a general in His army? If so, then some day, your name will be written in heaven.

Of course, God doesn't call all boys and girls to be generals in His army. He doesn't call all boys and girls to be priests and Sisters. He wants some of you to be fathers and mothers. He wants some of you to be doctors, lawyers, nurses, schoolteachers. Some of you will own your own business, and others will work in shops and factories. Some of you will have plenty of money, and others will be very poor.

God wants some of you, however, to work for Him. He wants some of you to help Him save souls. You know, there are millions of people who have never heard about God. Millions of people have never been baptized. They don't know how to pray. They have never gone to confession, and they have never received Jesus in Holy Communion. God wants these millions of people to know Him, love Him, and serve Him. It will be a big job to teach all of these people, and God wants some of you to help. Yes, God wants some of you to be Sisters and priests.

The life of a priest or Sister is not easy, but just think of all the good you can do. Why, every day of your life you will have any number of chances to do good. You will help people to live well, and you will help people to die well. Every day you will be helping people to get to heaven. If you will work for Christ, you will be the happiest person in this world. You will not only save your own soul, but you will help hundreds of others to save their souls.

Boys and girls, it is not too early to begin thinking about the future. God wants hundreds and thousands of priest and Sisters. Maybe, He wants you. My advice to you is to pray. Pray every day and ask God to lead you in the right direction. Ask His Blessed Mother, too, to watch over you and guide you. If you pray for that intention every day, I'm sure that, when you reach the eighth grade, you'll know pretty well just what God wants you to do.

If you feel that God wants you to be a priest or a nun, talk about it with the priest when you go to confession. Don't be afraid to go ahead! God wants you to be generous. If you are generous with God and offer to work for Him, God will give you plenty of help. With God's help you will succeed.

If God is calling you to be a priest or a nun, He wants to give you some very special graces. Don't turn God down! Don't refuse His graces! Remember, there may be a tablet in heaven waiting for your name. Don't leave your tablet blank! Have your name written in heaven!

25. The Magic Mirror

GEORGIE SPRINGER had a strange experience. Something happened to Georgie that doesn't happen to many sixth-grade boys. It was something that Georgie will never forget. Right now I must say that Georgie liked to have his own way. He didn't like to obey, and that's why Georgie got into trouble.

Georgie was a Boy Scout and one day last summer, Georgie's Scout troop went on a hike. Before the boys left on the hike, the scoutmaster told them to stay together. When they reached the park, the boys could separate into groups. At all times, each boy was to have a companion. No boy was ever to be alone.

When the boys reached the park, they made three bonfires and each boy cooked his own meal. Oh, they had a grand time and they had lots of fun. After the meal, the boys sang songs and some of them told stories. Then the scoutmaster ordered the boys to take a rest. Most of the boys obeyed and soon were sound asleep. But not Georgie Springer! Georgie pretended for a time that he was resting, and then he arose and tiptoed away to explore a near-by woods.

Georgie walked only a short distance in the woods

when something terrible happened. A tall man jumped out from behind a tree and caught Georgie by the arm. For a moment, Georgie was stunned and when he looked up into the man's face, he was terrified. Georgie knew the man and no wonder the boy was afraid. The tall man was the devil. Yes, the devil dressed in a red suit and a long, black cloak held Georgie's arm. The devil knew that Georgie was afraid and he laughed and sneered at the little boy.

"What do you want?" asked Georgie when he caught his breath.

The devil laughed. "I want you, Georgie," he answered. "I've wanted you for a long time and now I've got you."

"Please, let me go!" begged the little boy.

The devil shook his head. He refused to let the boy go. No, sir! The devil held Georgie's arm tightly because he didn't want the boy to get away.

Georgie pulled and tugged and even kicked the devil. But it was no use. The boy couldn't break away. Then, all of a sudden, Georgie had an idea.

"I've got seventeen cents in my pocket," said Georgie. "If you'll let me go, I'll give you all my money."

The devil refused Georgie's offer. The devil didn't want money. He wanted little Georgie.

"I'll give you my pocketknife, too. Please, let me go!" begged the boy.

"I don't need a pocketknife," answered the devil. "No, I won't let you go. You're coming with me."

The devil forced the boy to walk through the woods and Georgie Springer was awfully afraid. Some terrible thoughts ran through the boy's mind and he cried and sobbed, but the devil enjoyed making the boy suffer. Finally, Georgie made one more request.

"If I give you my magic mirror, will you let me go?"

The devil's eyes almost popped out of his head. "What's a magic mirror?" he asked.

Now Georgie didn't know it, but the devil had never seen a mirror. He had never seen a looking glass. Naturally, he was curious.

Georgie reached into his pocket and brought out his mirror. It was just a common, ordinary mirror, and there was nothing magic about it at all. The boy held up the mirror so that the devil could see.

When the devil looked into the mirror and saw that ugly face, he screamed and yelled. Why, the devil was so frightened that he forgot all about Georgie Springer. The devil ran through the woods like a streak of lightning and made a noise that was heard for miles. It all happened so quickly that Georgie could hardly believe his eyes. Yes, Georgie's mirror saved his life. His mirror saved him from the devil. Georgie's mirror chased the devil away.

Boys and girls, do you know that you have something that will chase away the devil? Oh, it's not a magic mirror, but it works much better than a magic mirror. What is it? It's holy water. Holy water, you know, is water blessed by a priest, and the devil hates holy water. Holy water will chase away the devil every time you use it, and you should use it often.

I have told you time and time again that the devil is always after you. He tempts you. He tries to get you to fall into sin. I know that he bothers you many times each day. If you will use some holy water, you'll get rid of the devil in a hurry. The next time you come to church, bring a little empty bottle with you and I'll give you some holy water. Then you'll have your own bottle of holy water and you can use it whenever you wish.

When should you use holy water? Every time you enter a church, make the sign of the cross with holy water on your fingers. Then the devil won't bother you while you're in church. Use some more holy water when you leave the church. Sprinkle it around your room at night, and use it in the morning when you say your prayers. Every time you enter or leave your room, make the sign of the cross with holy water. That's the way to get rid of the devil. Chase him every chance you get!

Children, you don't need a magic mirror to chase away the devil. Keep the devil away by using holy water!

26. The Boy Who Made God Smile

MEN WHO PRINT NEWSPAPERS receive many letters. They receive all kinds of letters every day. Some letters are letters of praise and others find fault.

The other day, the man who prints *The Evening News* received a very strange letter. The letter was from a little boy. The first time the man read the letter, he smiled. Then he read it again. Yes, the man read the letter several times. He liked the letter so much that he wanted to answer it, but how could he answer, when the boy didn't sign his full name to the letter? The boy didn't even say where he lived.

The newspaperman showed the letter to several of his friends and, when they read it, they smiled, too. All agreed that the letter should be put in the paper. Well, the newspaperman thought for a long time, and then, decided to print the boy's letter.

Thousands of people read the boy's letter in *The Evening News*. I suppose you are wondering what was in the boy's letter. Well, here's what it said:

Dear Sir:

I prayed to God to make my mother well and she got better. Please, say in the paper that I want to thank God. When God reads the paper, He will see it.

From a little boy who loves God,
Ernie

Now God sees everything and, when God read that little boy's letter in *The Evening News,* He smiled. He was very happy, too. Yes, God was pleased to find a boy who was thankful. Little Ernie prayed for something that he wanted very much. When God gave the boy just what he wanted, Ernie was right on the job to say, "Thanks."

It's too bad that there are not more children like little Ernie. You know, when most of us pray, we are always asking for something. We are always wanting something from God. But how many ever say a prayer of thanks? Oh, I'm afraid that there are not very many. Now that's too bad! When God gives us something, we should be right on the job to thank Him. We ought to say prayers of thanks just as often as we say prayers of asking. If we thank God for our blessings, then, the next time we want something, God will certainly hear our prayers and answer them more quickly.

When you do a favor for someone or give someone a present or share your candy with a friend, you expect your friend to be grateful and thank you. Isn't that right? Well, if your friend doesn't thank you, then you are not very anxious to do any more favors

103

for him. Now, I think that God feels the same way. When little boys and girls don't thank God, He isn't too anxious to answer their prayers the next time they call on Him. Remember that, children! You need God and you need His graces. When God is good to you, don't forget to thank Him!

Children, you have so many things for which you should be thankful. Thank God for your home, your parents, your brothers and sisters, your friends! Thank God for your strong bodies and for keeping you well! Thank Him for the food you eat and the clothes you wear! Thank God for helping you with your work in school! Thank Him every time you go to confession and when you receive Holy Communion! Oh, I could mention so many things for which you should be thankful, but I think that most of you know how good God is to you. Let God know that you thank Him for everything by saying prayers of thanks every day.

Too many boys and girls forget to thank God for their blessings. Little Ernie, however, didn't forget, and he made God very happy. You, too, can make God happy and show Him that you love Him by your prayers of thanks. Children, don't forget to say, "Thanks!"

27. Johnny's Invention

JOHNNY MORGAN was in the third grade of Our Lady of Mercy School. He was only eight years old, but he was very serious about his work in school. He worked hard, studied hard, and paid good attention to his teacher. Whenever Sister Clement wanted the third-grade children to do something, she always found Johnny Morgan right on the job to carry out her wishes. Johnny, you know, thought Sister Clement was just about tops.

It seems that Sister Clement was always telling the children to say their prayers. And that was one thing Johnny Morgan found hard to do. Johnny wanted to say his prayers every day but, somehow, he used to forget. He'd forget to pray in the morning and he'd forget to pray at night. Every time Sister Clement spoke to the children about saying their prayers, it bothered Johnny. The little fellow wanted to do the right thing but he always forgot to pray. Finally, Johnny decided to do something about it.

One morning recently Sister Clement was talking about prayer and, all of a sudden, Johnny Morgan raised his hand.

"Sister," said Johnny, "I don't forget my morning and night prayers any more. I made an invention."

"An invention?" smiled the Sister. "That's fine, Johnny! What kind of an invention is it?"

"Oh, I just took a piece of paper out of my tablet," answered the boy, "and pinned it up on the post of my bed."

"Just a piece of paper?" asked the Sister.

"Of course not," Johnny answered. "I wrote something on the paper."

"What did you write?" Sister Clement asked very solemnly.

The little boy seemed pleased. "Sister," he said, "I wrote up in the left-hand corner the words 'Jesus Christ,' and up in the right-hand corner I wrote 'The Devil.' You know, Sister, I'm having a contest between Jesus and the devil and I keep score on my paper. Every morning after I say my prayers, I mark one point for Jesus, and every night after I say my prayers, I mark another point for Jesus. If I don't say my prayers, then I have to give one point to the devil."

Sister Clement smiled and she was proud of little Johnny. "That's a fine invention," she said, "but tell me! Who is ahead in your contest?"

"Jesus is ahead," Johnny answered promptly. "Jesus is far ahead. He's got all the points, and the devil hasn't got any. When I wake up in the morning, the first thing I see is my score card and I say my prayers. When I get ready for bed, I see my score card again. My score card reminds me that I can't let Jesus down, so I say my prayers. I want Jesus to win."

Boys and girls, I think Johnny Morgan's invention was a pretty good idea and I'd like to pass along that idea to you this morning. What would happen if you had a sheet of paper before your eyes every morning and night? What would happen if you kept score on your prayers? Oh, I know what would happen. The same thing would happen to you that happened to Johnny Morgan — you wouldn't forget to say your prayers.

I know that you boys and girls want to say your prayers every day. But what happens to you? You forget, and you keep on forgetting day after day. Maybe you need a piece of paper pinned to your bed to remind you. I'll bet that piece of paper would work, and I'll bet, that if you would keep score, you would be saying your prayers every day. That little invention of Johnny's certainly worked for him, and it will work for you.

You know, children, Jesus and the devil are really in a race. They are both trying to win your soul. Every prayer you say puts Jesus ahead in the race and every prayer brings your soul closer to heaven. That's why you should pray often. That's why you should pray every day. If you don't pray, the devil will win the race and you won't go to heaven. You certainly don't want that to happen.

Don't neglect your prayers! Say your prayers every

morning and say them again at night! If you keep forgetting your prayers, then do what Johnny Morgan did! If necessary, keep score! Then you'll want to say your prayers every day. Johnny's invention is certainly worth trying. Isn't it? Well, I think so.

28. Denny Dinwit

IF I WERE TO ASK you which part of the newspaper you like best, I know what your answer would be. You would tell me that you like the funnies. I think most people read the funnies. Men, women, and children read the funnies and for some people the funnies are the best part of the newspaper. Now don't be surprised when I tell you that I read the funnies, too. Yes, I do! Of course, I don't read all the funnies, because some of them are not funny, but I do read the good ones.

Would you like to know which funnies I read? Well, I read "Blondie" because Blondie and her family are always good for a laugh. Then, I read "Little Henry" because he's everybody's favorite. "Joe Palooka" is on my list, too. I read "Bringing Up Father" because I know the man who draws Maggie and Jiggs, and I never miss "They'll Do It Every Time." Now there's one more funny that I certainly enjoy, and that is "Winnie Winkle."

Do you know why I read "Winnie Winkle"? Because I like the little fellow, Denny Dinwit. Little Denny Dinwit is one of my favorites. If you haven't followed little Denny in the past, then you had better get busy and meet him. Denny is a grand little fellow and you'll like him.

Wherever Denny Dinwit goes, a little green fellow follows him. The little green fellow is only about an inch tall and, most of the time, Denny doesn't see him and you don't see him, either. When Denny Dinwit is tempted to do wrong, however, the little green fellow appears immediately. When Denny is tempted to cheat, the little green fellow warns him that cheating is wrong. If Denny is tempted to tell a lie, the little green fellow holds him back. If Denny gets a job and wastes time, the little green fellow tells him that he must work for his pay. Yes, the little green fellow is always on the job, warning Denny Dinwit not to do wrong, warning him not to give in to temptation. Of course, Denny Dinwit always listens to the little green fellow and Denny always follows his advice. That's why Denny Dinwit always does the right thing.

Who is the little green fellow who follows Denny Dinwit wherever he goes? Who warns Denny and keeps him out of trouble? Well, you boys and girls who follow Denny know the answer. The little green fellow is Denny's conscience.

Now Denny Dinwit isn't the only one who has a conscience. You, too, have a conscience. Your conscience isn't a little green fellow because your conscience is inside of you. When the devil tempts you to do wrong, your conscience is always on the job.

Your conscience warns you and tells you what is right and what is wrong. If you will listen and follow the advice of your conscience, you'll never do wrong — you will always do the right thing.

Why do some boys and girls do wrong? Why do some boys and girls make sins? Because they stuff their ears and don't listen to their conscience. That's where they make a big mistake.

Almighty God wants boys and girls to do the right thing at all times. That's why God gave each of you a conscience. The little green fellow is Denny Dinwit's best friend, and *your* conscience is *your* best friend. Don't be annoyed when your conscience bothers you! When your conscience bothers you, that's a sign that you are in danger. If you will listen to and follow your conscience, you won't get into trouble, and you won't fall into sin.

Little Denny Dinwit doesn't look very bright in the funnies, but I think he is a very smart fellow. Denny never makes a mistake. He never does wrong. Denny always listens to and follows the advice of his conscience. Why don't you follow the example of little Denny Dinwit?

111

Index of Topics